THREE C
YEAR ONE

Anthology of the best new science fiction and fantasy from Three Crows Magazine

edited by

Alex Khlopenko and Olivia Hofer

THREE CROWS MAGAZINE
SCIENCE FICTION & FANTASY

Copyright © 2019 Three Crows Magazine

All rights reserved. No part of this book may be used or reproduced in any manner whatsoever without written permission except in the case of brief quotations embodied in critical articles or reviews.

This book is a work of fiction. Names, characters, businesses, organizations, places, events and incidents either are the product of the author's imagination or are used fictitiously. Any resemblance to actual persons, living or dead, events, or locales is entirely coincidental.

For information contact :
editor@threecrowsmagazine.com
http://threecrowsmagazine.com

ISBN 9781079110050

Book design by Alex Khlopenko
Cover Art by Cze Peku

First Edition: August 2019

10 9 8 7 6 5 4 3 2 1

Contents

Foreword by Michael R. Fletcher

"High, High Country" by Brandon Daubs 1

"Riggers" by RJ Barker 15

"Animals of Ure" by Daryna Stremetska 27

"Necessary Evil" by Anna K. Scott 43

"Deciding Vote" by Michael Kellichner 51

"Diplomatic Immunity" by Daniel M. Kimmel 65

"In Cube Eight" by Steven Couch 79

"Stones" by Anna Smith Spark 97

"Knowing Your Type" by Eliza Chan 113

"Little Bear" by Avra Margariti 127

"Till the Very End of Days" by T.A. Sola 135

"Redundancy of Yellow Flower Tea" by Luke Frostick 149

"The Necromancer's Garden" by Gerard Mullan 161

"Fathom" by J.S. Rogers 177

"Folk Hunters" by Kate Karl Lanier 197

About the Authors 205

Acknowledgments 208

Foreword

by Michael R. Fletcher

You have to be some kind of crazy to want to edit and publish a fantasy magazine. Let's face it, the endeavour isn't exactly a get-rich-quick scheme. Hell, it's probably closer to a haemorrhage-money-like-someone-shanked-your-carotid scheme.

And yet here they are. Crows. Three of them.

Let's back up a bit.

I first noticed THREE CROWS on my twitter feed back in early 2018. I watched them go through a few iterations of their logo, hunting for exactly the right look. I saw them put out the call for stories and even interviewed a couple of highly questionable writers. When they began publishing reviews, I eyed them like a Canadian spotting a bowl of the finest lobster poutine.

I knew then they were doomed.

With each episode they're a step closer to their dark fate. The production quality increases. They're taking on bigger projects, receiving more books from writers desperate for reviews. More interviews. More art. More stories. More reviews. More... you get it. They even have a slush pile, that stack of books and stories they just haven't got to yet. The only consolation writers get from being in the slush pile is that some day it will get so tall it'll fall over and crush the editor in question.

Who would want this? Who would torture themselves with deadlines, wading through endless stories about magical armpits, and chatting with drooling alcoholics in the hopes they'll say something interesting? Did you know most writers have a weaker grasp of the rules of grammar than the average lawyer?

Why!? Why would you want this?!?!?

Clearly it's a labour of love. Love and madness. Or maybe love of madness.

A year on and THREE CROWS is better than ever. Still growing. Still striving. Still championing this mad little corner of the publishing world.

And so let's raise a pint (yes, whiskey comes in pints) and toast the good folks of THREE CROWS. Cheers to the editor! Cheers to the reviewers and interviewers! Cheers to the artists! Cheers to whoever that is in the gimp suit reading the slush pile!

I look forward to the next year!

Cheers!

High, High Country

by Brandon Daubs

You ever seen lightning that color, Phil? Doesn't look right, does it? Watch the trees over the ridge there. You'll see it again. Lightning just doesn't have a reason to be that kind of color and it doesn't have a reason to be hitting that same spot over and over, either.

Oh, hell. Don't look so worried. We're safe here in the station. Probably. You know how the old marshal used to pass the time when we got stuck in a storm just like this one?

You guessed it. It's story time.

Listen to that rain, Phil. Listen to the wind howl through that crack in the door which, by the way, I told you to fix last summer. What do we pay you for? Measuring bear shit? Anyway, on a night just like this a park ranger from the

Portal where all those car campers pluck fish out of a stocked pond realized he might be a bit out of his depth away from all that, at least a hundred miles deep into the high country. Let's call him Earl. He was getting a little older even then, with knees that didn't work quite like they used to, sunken knuckles, a little curve to his back and black stubble going white all over the place.

He was a mean old shit, this Earl. He wasn't any kind of "can I see your permit please" park ranger. He had a nice easy gig, watching the parking lot at the Portal most times, and he got bored of it. He wanted to go for a little jaunt out deep into the mountains.

Boy, was that a mistake.

Not too far over the first few passes, the storm hit. Winds whipping at 60 miles or more. Hail stripping poor Earl's scalp clean off, just about. The whole thing came out of nowhere from a clear blue sky, so quick it was a wonder he got down off the pass before the lightning started. We lost a Scout to that storm. Lightning took a fat branch off a pine and it crushed one of the poor little dudes in his sleep, right through his tent. Sometimes people die out here, Phil, but we don't ever like for it to be one of them.

Yeah, I know that really happened.

We are telling stories, Phil. Don't look so worried. Just listen.

Earl found some cover in a bunch of trees and he was hunkered down when the woman appeared. She drifted through the trees and out of the hail like the wind whipping her hair around and around was just a nice summer breeze. Lightning crashed behind her and Earl saw a face that made his breath stick in his throat.

"Help me," she said. Hail hit her and bounced off.

"Come in out of the storm, ma'am," said Earl, with a gesture toward the little shelter he had set up. He offered a cup of hot coffee with more than a little schnapps thrown in there.

This woman couldn't find her kid, she said. Little lad, maybe 13 or so.

Earl asked if they were with the Scouts. She looked deep into his eyes for a long time and Earl got this real weird feeling, like someone had just spun his brain all the way around.

"Yes," she said.

Earl assured this lady that he would find her kid, but he wasn't optimistic. He thought maybe a bear had got him, or a cougar. Maybe he had slipped and fallen. Earl didn't want to think these things—like I said, rangers don't ever like to lose a Scout—but he couldn't help it.

Probably a bear this high up, he decided.

It wasn't any kind of bear, Phil. I'll spoil that for you straight off.

Take a look at that lightning out there, huh? Crazy color. I bet you've never seen lightning like that in all your days.

Neither had Earl.

* * *

In the morning the storm didn't quite let up but the hail had turned into a soft rain, at least, and the winds died down enough that Earl didn't feel he might be thrown off his feet any second. He checked on the woman bundled up in his little shelter, drank a cup of his special coffee, counted out the shells for the .44 stuffed into the top of his bag and set out in the direction of the woman's last camp.

Yeah, I know a Magnum isn't exactly park ranger regulation—but I already told you, Earl wasn't any kind of regulation park ranger.

The first thing he noticed was the valley. Now, you know campers like I do, Phil. If you don't put up a shitload of signs with huge red letters they'll camp anywhere—and I do mean anywhere. Ten feet from a cliff. Miles from water, or even smack in the middle of a goddam marsh, with ground as wet as a baby's ass. This place was on a whole other level. If the woman hadn't told Earl about this little valley, he would never have found it on the other side of a rather fetid little pond. The path wormed behind a big pile of rocks covered in manzanita and once he got up past all that, the place was totally still.

Not a sound. No wind. No chittering squirrels. Not even the rain made a sound against the rocks or the dirt.

Earl never did find the woman's camp, but he did find a nice big pile of bear shit and tracks leading up some rocks into the dark mouth of a cave. The rocks looked a little weird here, I might add. Kinda burned. Campers lit fires wherever they pleased, Earl decided, but even so he wasn't about to hop in that cave sober. He drained what was left in his flask, loosened the bag around his shoulder and flicked on a flashlight before he stepped down into the dark.

Schnapps, of course. I got some right here. Yeah, sure. Get the glasses.

Cheers! Now pay attention.

The cave went a little farther back and a little farther down than most caves in the high country. Not all of them are like the California Caverns, you know, with long twisting passages and stalactites and all that crap, but this one was. The rocks started to look a little strange, too—

shiny almost, like metal. Some of them reflected the light from Earl's flashlight with little lights of their own and the floor was awful smooth, like the bottom of a lava tube. At the end of it all was a little crack in the wall, and through that Earl found himself in a cave almost perfectly round, like someone had measured before cutting it out.

It was in this place that he found the bear, backed into the far side of the chamber, looking right at him. Its fur didn't look quite right. It had dark eyes fixed on Earl already like it had known he was coming. It didn't bob or weave its head back and forth like a pissed off real bear would have. It didn't grunt or stand up. It just stood there, surrounded by...something.

Bones. Little bones. Larger bones that might have belonged to a dog. And also, bones topped with skulls that might have had faces attached at one time.

People bones.

Oooh. I know. Scary, right? Just wait.

About the time Earl began to wonder what in the hell kind of bear this was, glaring at him with black eyes from the far end of the chamber, the thing began to change. Those eyes widened and bulged out of its head until they raised up like the stalks of some kind of slug. Its jaw unhinged and stretched almost to the floor and tongues snaked out— that's what I said, tongues, as in more than one, reaching out for Earl even from that far away. Earl shit his pants. No shame in that. He dropped his flashlight and whipped his bag off his shoulder but before he could reach inside, that thing had him. It ripped the bag out of his hands and wrapped those tongues around his arms and legs and he had just enough time to see the pile of half-eaten fur and mess that might have been a real bear at one point, before the eyes of the thing drew him in.

You know frog eyes, Phil? Or the eyes of a goat? You ever look at 'em for a second?

Pretty freaky-deaky, right?

Those eyes aren't anything compared to the eyes of this thing. They whirled and moved and switched colors and Earl could feel his brain spinning around and around in his head like it had with the woman for a second, but a thousand times worse. He remembered his time in the Gulf War and all the friends he'd lost to bombs or people he'd killed. He remembered scratching the ear of his dog Chomper while the old mongrel breathed its last breath and looked up at Earl with clouded eyes still so full of trust. He remembered his dear old dad with a hand around his neck, squeezing until mom smashed him over the head with a cutting board.

Earl remembered these things and more, all the worst things, a thousand times in a single second and the seconds passed. One. Two. Three.

I don't know what it was that saved Earl from bat-shit insanity. Maybe he was tough upstairs as well as on the outside. Maybe God stepped in. Maybe he was just too drunk to really comprehend all the hate and pain and misery whirling through his brain in that instant but whatever it was, Earl found a new shape by the chewed-on corpse of the bear, a shape in a blue uniform, a shape like a knocked-out little dude.

The kid. Earl remembered why he was here—the woman. Her boy.

The kid didn't look hurt. But even if he was, Earl had to call a chopper. He had to get that body out of here. Somehow, Earl got a hunting knife in his hand. He cut at the tongues holding him and when he hit the ground, he bashed his face pretty good but he was focused.

The bag. He had to reach his bag.

God, Earl had never felt his arms were so fuckin' short in all his life until just then, as he reached bloody fingers out for his bag while the whatever-it-was thrashed and finally made a sound, a shriek like a thousand dying cats. A new mess of tongues shot out of its mouth toward Earl but he whipped out his Magnum and as many shells as he could carry in one fist, and fired blind behind him while he ran screaming out of the cavern through the dark, out through the burned valley and around the fetid pond, back up the mountain to his camp and up a tree where he huddled in the branches drooling like a monkey scared out of its goddam mind.

I don't know if he killed the whatever-it-was, Phil. Maybe he did—or, maybe it's still out there. You'll have to let me finish my story.

Here, have another drink.

✳ ✳ ✳

The woman woke up and Earl screamed when she climbed out of their little makeshift shelter and called up to him. He had forgotten all about her. The rain had stopped but lightning still flashed over the not-so-distant valley and a deep cold had set in, the kind of cold you only get in the high country. Earl found himself shivering so bad that when he finally got control of himself and tried to climb down from the tree to speak with the woman, he slipped and almost broke his arm clean in half when he hit the ground.

He thought he had, but the woman bent to lay hands

on his arm and Earl felt a warmth like the glow of a good campfire flow through him until the pain died down.

"It's only sprained," she said, and then, "Earl...I'm sorry. I didn't know."

Earl didn't respond. He pushed himself up into a sitting position and opened his white-knuckled fist to count the .44 shells that were still clutched tight in there. Three. He flipped open the chamber on his Magnum.

None.

He started to load. His hands shook so bad he could barely hold the shells. The woman watched him for a while before she asked, "What are you doing?"

"I'm going back in there." Earl thought somebody else must have said this for him, but it was out there, now. He had to commit. One shell went in. Two.

The woman stopped him with her hand on the third shell.

"I can sense your fear," she said. "You're still going back?"

Earl liked her eyes. He saw warmth and compassion. He saw concern. Most of all, he saw the pain of a mother whose child was still out there, somewhere, in danger.

"People die out here, sometimes," Earl said. "But we don't like for it to be a Scout."

Yeah, you think you know where this is going next, huh Phil? Get your mind out of the gutter. I know it was you who put that Heavy Metal calendar up on the wall.

Just listen, and try not to get too excited.

The woman slid Earl's third .44 shell down the neck of her Under Armour.

She pressed her lips against Earl's and he remembered two details in this moment more than any others—the sense of peace, in spite of all he'd been through in the last day or so, and the warmth that soaked through the woman's skin into his. When they finally pulled apart, Earl caught the woman's gaze and remembered all sorts of things he had forgotten. He remembered the first time he'd kissed a girl behind the bleachers at his school. He remembered his mother singing happy birthday and the feel of the wind through the open window of his jeep.

"I didn't know quite what we were dealing with before," said the woman, and she plucked Earl's .44 shell from the neck of her shirt to give it back. Earl held it for a moment and watched the way a weird new light danced beneath the metal. "I thought maybe my boy had just gotten lost. I didn't expect it to be...this."

The woman paused for a moment.

"I know you can get him back," she whispered.

Earl shoved the glowing shell into his Magnum and snapped the chamber shut. He said nothing. He just turned, and began the hike back down to the burned out valley.

Because remember, I told you.

Earl wasn't any kind of regulation park ranger.

***

Pow! Haha, you like that one, huh Phil? Made you jump right out of your pants. Hey, don't look at me like that. You're cleaning up your own mess if you piss yourself. That thunder's getting closer. I guess I'd better hurry it up, before it tears this place down.

When Earl returned to the cave, the whatever-it-was seemed surprised. It actually made a sound as it swiveled a shapeless head around to stare, dragging its long jaw on the ground. Earl tried not to comprehend how ugly this thing was. His knees shook. His Magnum rattled in his grip but at least, for whatever reason, the thing hadn't seen him coming this time.

The bones of the real bear had been picked clean, and the whatever-it-was had dragged the kid in the uniform over to its feet. Whatever Earl did, he would have to do it, fast.

He raised his Magnum.

And he fired, at the exact second the thing's eyes began to change, and Earl felt his brains going again the way of a stirred slushie.

You ever see those old picture-within-a-pictures that were popular in the 70s, the ones that if you looked at them real close just went on forever and ever? Yeah, like the cover of that Pink Floyd album we've got in the other room? The Droste Effect, I think it's called. Well, what happened next was something like that. Earl stared into the eyes of that thing and the shell from his Magnum sank into the goo of its face and the light turned its eyes to look at each other, as well as at him. Earl found himself lost in his own memories of the war, of his father, of his many other miseries…but also thrown in there were a whole mess of new horrors.

Earl felt pain all over, as a mob of hideous shapes jabbed and pulled him with hooks sunk into his flesh away from a familiar burrow and into some sort of crate.

An eternity of dark and cold came after. When the darkness finally lifted, Earl felt fear inside of some unfamiliar place as the hideous shapes screamed and flailed all around him. Walls and floors split open. Alarms screamed in pitches that made his ears ring and he began to see stars through the fractured hull of wherever he was. Earl remembered flame, flame everywhere cooking him alive, and an impact that left him broken and half-mad with pain. Earl knew this memory wasn't his. The only familiar part had been the mountain, and a nice view of a secluded valley—the same burned-up valley he had climbed up into, just a few minutes before.

This thing hadn't come from the high country at all, Earl knew.

It came from the high, high country.

Yeah, fuckin' outer space, Phil. Do I have to spell it out for you? It doesn't really matter where it came from anyway, though, does it? It was here.

Have some more schnapps. We're almost done.

On and on this went, a memory within a memory within a memory, until the creature shrieked and turned its eyes away from each other with such force they seemed to break open and ooze red down its face. Earl's glowing magnum shell shone brighter and a moment before he thought he might rip out his own eyes as well, his memories changed.

The light from that shell brought Earl back from the edge in the same way it blinded the whatever-it-was. He went through a whole host of good stuff, stuff that left him feeling warm inside for a long time after. Most of all he remembered his time with the woman back at his camp— the feel of her lips, the taste of her, the warmth of her skin against his—the way she had looked deep into his eyes when he'd made up his mind to come back to the cave.

He raised up his Magnum again and plugged the creature two more times right in the face. He jumped forward and heaved the kid over one shoulder—and he got the fuck out of there, pursued by the sounds of a thousand eternal torments.

* * *

It's just a story, Phil. Take it easy. Lightning's getting pretty crazy outside though, huh?

Hey, do me a favor. Go to that drawer. Open it up.

Yeah, I know there's a Magnum in there. Bring it to me.

Quit shaking so damn much! You're going to drop it. I need you to go through the shells in there, too. They've gotten a little jumbled, over the years. Pick out the ones with a brighter tip while I finish up.

I don't know what happened to the woman and her kid after that. Earl returned to his camp with the little Scout in tow. Little dude didn't say much the whole way—he was dazed from his time in the caves, I think—but he lit right up when he saw his mom, huddled over the campfire. Earl had never seen more tears or hugging in all his life. He spent a few more nights with them at a nearby lake, until the night of that meteor storm we had a few years back. Earl looked up at all the shooting stars and when he looked back down, he was alone.

Just like that. Still, those were the best few days of my life, I think.

I mean his life. Earl's life.

Give me the rest of the schnapps—and the cup. The big cup.

Ok, I think that's everything. The story's over, Phil, so listen up.

I'm going outside.

Yeah, I noticed it's still storming balls out there. Yeah, that lightning has gotten pretty goddam close. Try to focus. I'm going outside, and I don't know how long I'll be gone. Turn off the lights. Bolt the door. Yes, all the bolts. When I get back, I will knock on that door three times and I will tell you the following.

Earl wasn't any kind of regulation park ranger.

If you don't hear me say those exact words in that exact order, Phil, I want you to stay very still. I want you to creep to a dark place and stay there. Don't make a sound. Don't turn the lights on. Because whatever the fuck it is out there yelling and banging on that door if it doesn't say those words exactly the way I said them just now, it isn't me. Trust me and God above when I say you do not want that thing in here with you.

Jesus, Phil! Take a breath, man, you look like you're about to pass out! I was just pulling your leg. There's nothing out there for you to worry about. A bear, maybe. You don't need to act so scared, like a rat in the tiger cage.

Unless I don't come back.

If I don't come back, you can be just as scared as you want.

Riggers

by RJ Barker

We look after our own in this circus.
As long as I'm ringmaster we always will.
The Riggers turned up at the camp one morning as we were starting to erect the Big Top.

Anywhere else there would have been screaming, running, fear, panic, but this is the Circus, strange is every day. Five black figures strode out of the morning mist, buzzing at each other as they came to stop in front of the tent we'd spent hours laying out. They stood there; it was something about their arms and legs that upset me most of all, too long, too spindly. Too strange.

We tried to make them go away but they didn't want to.
Andre, our strong man, ended up with a broken arm; snapped with such contemptuous ease that we knew, if they

had really wanted to, they could have killed him. One flick of a triple elbowed, black carapaced appendage left Andre's arm hanging uselessly at his side.

He screamed a lot.

Andre is a big man, ex-army and with a history of violence that had forced him away from the public and into our arms. He'd never lifted a finger against us, he was our protector, and with him beaten so easily we had few choices but to withdraw. Walk away and gather in small groups to curse and mutter. A couple of the crew suggested calling the police but that was never going to happen.

We look after our own, we sort out our own problems.

Outsiders make things worse.

Tommy the Dwarf noticed what they were doing first. Although we never mean to ignore Tommy, he always seems to be on the outskirts of our conversations. Even within the tight-knit group of dwarves, he's shunned a little as if he makes them uncomfortable. He's not the brightest, or nicest of buttons our Tommy, but we still love him.

"Look at what the fucking bastards are doing!" he shouted. Tommy swears all the time, as though he thinks his rough language can increase his mental stature.

The creatures were putting up our tent. Buzzing at each other from deep within those shining, black, barrel-chested bodies as they worked. One of them lifted the main tent pole, a task that usually took twenty of us pulling and sweating and heaving together. The four other creatures scrambled up the pole, holding thick steel mooring wires in chittered hands and buzzing in harmony.

The sound hurt my ears.

We drank bad coffee and watched as the creatures put up our tent in a third of the time it would usually take us. With that done they stayed aloft, hiding in the rafters among the web of high-tension cables. We didn't know how to get them down and they seemed happy up there.

We went ahead with rehearsals as planned.

What else could we do?

"We always wanted to hire some fucking bastard riggers anyway," said Tommy the Dwarf, then he stared up into the heights of the tent, "fucking bastards."

The Riggers didn't bother us as we rehearsed so we decided to leave them up there. Not that we had a choice. Working out how to get them down could wait until it came to de-rigging the tent and besides, we had a show to put on.

There's a right time for all things.

During the performance that night we discovered that the Riggers were territorial. Ellie, the trapeze artist went up in one of her arcing swings and never came down. At first, the audience became hushed, only the odd cough or screaming child breaking the silence as we waited. A scattering of nervous laughter pattered around the tent until, with a deft bow, a practiced smile and a crack of my whip I turned it into a deafening round of applause. You never let the audience know that anything is wrong. Up above me something with compound eyes the size of my head stared down from its place in the heights of the tent.

Ellie would have enjoyed the acclaim.

It was how she would have wanted to go.

The Riggers don't have faces, just what looks like a tall and thin triangular mass of compacted hair, two small tentacles, in constant motion, stick out from the front of it and their massive compound eyes are slightly offset from each other; one half-way up the triangle of their head, the other slightly higher. The lack of symmetry gives them a sense of menace that's difficult to explain if you haven't seen them. But it is there.

They are unsettling to look at, but so am I, if you get too close. My scars are mostly healed but you can see the thin web of white raised flesh that covers my skin. If you get near enough to look.

Which you won't.

No one spoke to me about what had happened. Ellie had never been popular, the trapeze artists are often difficult to get on with and like to position themselves outside the tightly knit community of the circus. It's a terrible joke but they are a highly strung breed. My mother and father were a trapeze act. I had heard that their circus had recently closed.

It's difficult not to smile when I think of them being out of work.

Ellie's husband, Joachim, was gone the next morning, he didn't take any of his things. We burned his clothes and doled out the rest of his possessions amongst us, it's the way things are done.

For the dead.

When it was time to move on the Riggers seemed to know, I don't know how but they did. They brought down the tent and left it laid out as they had found it when they appeared.

Woven around the main pole was a thick band of brown hair.

Ellie's hair had been brown.

We burnt the hair and the Riggers took over her empty caravan.

At the next town, we hired on a trampolinist.

Sometimes, on the nights when we are stopped between

towns, I peer in through the window of the Rigger's caravan. The interior is covered in grey webbing and along its length pulse small, blue lights. On the webbing are suspended the Riggers. They have humanoid shapes but the absolute black of their shells turns them into floating silhouettes against the pulsing light. It looks as though someone has casually strewn them around the interior of the caravan, some upside down, some sideways, as if gravity has no hold on them.

When they first arrived we feared them because they were alien. It's natural. But after a time you learn to accept almost anything and get on with your life.

I learned that when I was a young girl.

Now the Riggers always put the tent up. We have to lay it out for them, but it's still a much easier task than putting the thing up ourselves. In exchange for putting the tent up, they get to live in the rafters during performances. They seem happy, sometimes we hear them buzzing to each other. I wish I knew what it meant.

The trampolinist lasted one show before she bounced just that bit too high. I'm glad we hadn't had time to get to know her that well.

We tried all manner of the more spectacular acts, but it always ended unfortunately.

Our circus appeared in the newspaper. They referred to us as the "Bermuda Triangle of Entertainment." That brought us a lot more customers, but of course, it also brought the police. Always a problem. Not all of the circus people have visas or work permits so our staff halves when the police arrive.

It was a familiar experience: to walk around with the policeman while his men searched the caravans for evidence of foul play, all the while smiling and pretending nothing was wrong.

When we walked toward the Riggers' caravan I tried to act normal whilst thinking of some sort of excuse or way of explaining them away. They buzzed more loudly than usual and I wished they would stop, it was sure to attract attention and made me feel like my head was about to explode. The policeman walked straight past the caravan. The only sign he made of being aware of something was to bat around his head with a hand, as if at a mosquito.

"Damn flies," he said, as he motioned his men back to their cars. "You got any runaways hiding here? You should tell us if you have, it'll go badly for you if we come back one day and find something."

"Just me," I said and my face flushed with guilt. My younger sister would be fifteen now.

"Was that a joke?" he asked.

I said nothing. Sometimes it's best to stay quiet and hope no one notices you. The policeman shrugged his shoulders and left. Human Cannonball joined us without an invitation. He wasn't a circus person, he was a man bent on fame who saw us as a vehicle to amplify his own profile after reading about us in the paper. He laughed at the dwarves, he made fun of Oswald, the hunch-backed dog trainer, and he had no respect for me, his ringmaster. He was a big man who called himself Orlok, he'd heard it in a film somewhere and thought it sounded exotic. In reality, he was from a small provincial town and had no talent other than being hurled from a gun, and an innate ability to bully people he knew could not strike back.

Usually, Andre would deal with such people. But Orlok had come forewarned and with stories about how immigration dealt with those wanted for crimes in other countries. Andre went pale and wouldn't approach Orlok. He said his broken arm was still healing and there was nothing he could do. He could still lift his weights though.

I wondered what Andre had done and then realized it didn't matter, he was one of us now.

Orlok didn't get up early enough to help with the tent, so he never saw the Riggers. As the policeman, he was unaware of their caravan. He considered himself our big draw since we had no high wire acts. What happened was inevitable really.

He wouldn't listen.

We talked to him about low trajectories and how bad things might happen if he tried to go too high.

"You're circus people and you're superstitious," he flicked an imaginary something off his shoulder, barely bothering to acknowledge me, "I can't abide by them, I got records to break." He turned away from me to smear more oil on his bare, well-muscled chest.

That night the "Bermuda Triangle of Entertainment" claimed another victim. I can't say I would have lost too much sleep about it if I hadn't changed my usual routine.

When the audience had left I wandered into the performers' circle and sat down. As a rule, after sunset, we don't go into the top. We're not forbidden to, if you don't go too high, the Riggers don't seem to care, but still, the big top is a dark place and who knows what might happen in the dark?

A drunk man: Heavy fists. A laughing woman. A crying baby.

I don't like the dark.

I sat in the front row, earlier a large group of children

had been seated there. They had laughed and smiled all the way through the show.

Children should laugh and smile. It's very important to me.

As I sat there, I heard a noise above the constant creak of canvas and wood, as the tent strained against the wind. It wasn't the strange hum of the Riggers talking to one another, something different, something alien.

Whimpering.

Human whimpering, a piteous sound. If a dog was making that sound I'd have shot it. I walked to the center of the ring, damp sawdust squeaking under my boots, and looked up. Out of the darkness fell an object, fluttering and twisting in the air, a strange snowflake that landed to glint up at me from the dirty sawdust, a crescent of moisture on one rounded end.

A single human fingernail.

I picked it up and returned to my seat on the front row wondering what to do and eventually deciding on nothing. I watched a spider weave its web on the chair in front of me until it crouched down in the center, waiting for food to fly into its trap.

The whimpering from above went on for a long time.

Eventually, I left. Thoughts of human whimpering. Thoughts of another me and another circus on my mind. Thoughts of all those performers who'd never interfered when the fists were flying.

Circus people are always looking for work.

The Riggers were totally uninterested in everything around them, uninterested to the point of being oblivious. One day a Rigger stepped on one of the Oswalds' trained dogs as it walked back to its caravan after packing up.

There was no malice in what the Rigger did. It didn't do it on purpose or to hurt the dog, it was as if the dog wasn't there for it. The same way they act around anyone who doesn't infringe on their territory. One hard black foot landed on the dog, it didn't even peer down with its great off-set, compound eyes. There was an audible "Snap!" as the carapaced foot crushed the animal's spine.

The Rigger walked, on leaving the crippled animal screaming in pain and Oswald crying for his dog. Andre took a barbell and put the little creature out of its misery with a swift downward stroke. Oswald screamed and cried. Consumed by grief, he started after the Rigger but I grabbed him and held him back. He shrugged me off and stood alone, shaking and weeping to himself. A long time ago he'd withdrawn from human contact, his deformity making him shun most people, but he loved his dogs like they were his children.

He kept them safe.

Parents should keep their children safe.

"This can't go on, we need to get rid of them, we need to. They are murderers," he hissed.

Expulsion from the circus requires all of our input. A meeting. This one was especially rowdy, some fought for the Riggers, how useful they were, how they asked nothing and gave their strength. Others wanted them dead. Oswald led this faction, still crying. All hell broke loose when Andre told us he knew people who could get us guns if we needed them.

No one mentioned the trampolinist, or Ellie, or Orlok, but they were outraged about the dog.

They are not bad people, my circus crew. They were scared and to tell the truth so was I. The Riggers were so unlike us, and it was hard not to wonder what was going on behind those expressionless compound eyes. Most days I tried not to think about them. The meeting ended deadlocked, and as is always the case when they don't know where to turn, they looked to me.

Ringmaster, in and out of the ring.

I needed to walk and think. I told them so and they sat back to wait.

I had the fingernail in my pocket. I took it out and looked at it. It was a symbol of pain. They hadn't hurt anyone I really cared about, yet, but who knew what they would do?

Buzzing floated through the still night air and I followed the sound.

It came from the far side of the tent, near the animal cages. The sound as the Rigger's foot snapped the dog's spine sprang into my mind, I ran. Without a High Wire act, the animals were our big draw now.

All five Riggers stood in front of the bear's cage. They held, what passed for them as, hands as they hummed. The bear was unharmed and pacing backward and forwards in its usual endless stalking of imaginary prey. After a few moments, the Riggers seemed to slump slightly and the towering black figures moved on to the chimps. They ignored the horses and the dogs, all the animals that were native to this country were passed by.

The way the Riggers hummed, it seemed mournful, lost.

My decision was made then amongst the animals, as I listened to the Riggers sing a sad, lost song. No one should be alone, everyone needs some sort of family, a place they can be safe. Somewhere to be a home, when your real home is somewhere you can never go back to.

The Riggers were part of our family now.

Maybe it was time we got a new trapeze act.

I wondered whether my mother or father would recognize me after ten years.

I had a letter to write, a job offer to send.

I wondered whether my sister would be scared too. I hoped she wasn't too damaged.

A family reunion to organize.

I would have to find a way to keep her off the trapeze though.

We look after our own in this circus.

As long as I'm ringmaster we always will.

Animals of Ure

By Daryna Stremetska

English Translation by Maksym Bakalov

The air in the space suit tasted of rubber. It wasn't a big deal — they were almost certain that the atmosphere of Ure was suitable for humans. They only put their space suits on as a precaution. According to the Royal Archive, it's been 20 years since servants of His Majesty Ludwig CVIII set foot on this planet. Who knows what may have changed.

The hatch of the spaceship opened with a pshh, and for an instant, the astronauts were blinded by the shining green. Ariel, keen to get the feel of real, non-metallic land under his feet, got out. He was short, and the grass reached his waist. The long beep of the space suit sensor indicated that the air was suitable for breathing, and he pulled off his helmet. His lungs filled with the humid air of Ure. For a moment, Ariel felt sorry for the two carybaras who had to leave this beautiful planet and spend the rest of their lives on the desert-like Kare. But such was His Majesty's will.

"Hey!" Greg said through the helmet. "Are you going to pick up your equipment? The day's four hours shorter here, you know."

"Coming," said Ariel, but before turning back, he looked up at the forest that stretched wide like a wall. The forest looked back at him. Its eyes were neither kind nor evil. Only wary. The carybara who had watched their landing also showed little emotion. But he sure knew what he was going to do.

***

"Okay, one more time," said Greg, while Ariel checked his equipment. "Zoologist told me that there are no big animals here, except for our pair of relict carybaras, but there are a few species of bitey insects. Our 'friends' should be good-natured and primitive, but I wouldn't really count on that, so take this," he tossed one of the stun guns to Ariel and showed him his net-equipped handcuffs.

"Have you checked the interpreters?" asked Ariel.

"Yes. Mine is acting up, so you will do the talking. Let's go."

When they entered the forest, there were still ten hours until the sunset. In that time, they had to reach the rock somewhere inside the forest where the carybaras lived, fetch them and take them back to the ship. However, they could face a few problems. One — the carybaras may not be there. Or anywhere. If this happens, they would have to spend at least a week there, and even that may not save them from the anger of His Majesty. Carybaras had to be brought back. And two — they may not get there by sunset. In that case... well, in that case, they would see. Maybe they would spend the night in a cave.

"And besides," said Greg, "they're a male and a female. How can we be sure we aren't marching towards a bunch of crazy herbivores?"

"They live very long," Ariel said. "So long, in fact, that they have seen severe climate change which made them barren," he added, thinking to himself, "Maybe they're even lucky that we're taking them with us. Maybe the climate of Kare will suit them better."

The trees grew thick, and here and there they had to use lasers to get through, but the further they went, the clearer it got. At last, feeling like they broke through a wall, Ariel and Greg found themselves in a sort of a courtyard where there was now some room to move. It was getting hot, but that was not the problem. The insects were. They swarmed, they buzzed, they flew right in your face. The visors helped, of course, but you still had to wipe them every now and then.

A third of their time had passed. The rock was now about half an hour away, and they decided to take a break. Greg turned on his ultrasonic repellent, which was supposed to fend off the insects but barely did so. Ariel opened his lunchbox and took out a snake paste sandwich.

"Ureo o?" said someone on the left. Ariel dropped his sandwich on the ground and a big ant immediately crawled on top of it. In the bushes beside them stood one of the carybaras. Greg started up and aimed his automatic net. His other hand was resting on the stun gun. Ariel activated his interpreter just in time to avert a fight.

"Can I have one?" repeated the animal. She stepped out

of the bush, and they now saw her pretty white red-spotted fur.

"We... yes, of course."

Ariel reached into his lunchbox for another sandwich, but carybara said, "Can I have the one on the ground?" She thought about it for a moment and added, "Please?"

Ariel signaled to Greg, and he sat back down.

The three of them ate. At first, it was just Ariel and the carybara, but soon enough Greg joined them too. He was still tense, though everything seemed to be going smoothly. Then the carybara asked them, "You're scientists, right? Do you want to see how I live? My name is Doré."

"Nice to meet you, Doré," said Ariel. "I'm Ariel and this is Greg. He can't speak with you, because his voice interpreter is broken, but he can understand us."

He didn't say if they were scientists or not, but that didn't seem to bother the animal. She looked over at Greg and said, "Hi, Greg." He gave her a thin smile.

On their way to the rock, Doré took the lead. She would often run ahead of them, and they had to follow her by the red spots on her back that showed between the trees from time to time.

"I thought you said they were herbivores," said Greg.

"She didn't know it was snake paste," shrugged Ariel.

"We should've used the net while she was close," he insisted.

"Yeah, and then we'd never see the other carybara," argued Ariel. "We're doing everything right."

They reached the rock. Doré was nowhere to be seen.

"Where are you, Doré?" Ariel called.

No reply. Greg gave Ariel a questioning look. He called again. They decided to round the rock and explore.

"Look!" said Ariel and pointed up.

There was a cave mouth, with a winding path leading up to it from behind the rock.

"Oh, you're here already," said Doré from behind, startling Greg.

"Where the hell have you been?!"

Doré looked at him confused.

"I don't understand your friend. What did he say?"

Ariel eyed Greg with a disapproving look and mouthed, "Good-natured." Then he turned to Doré.

"He was worried that you disappeared. Do you live in that cave?" he pointed up.

Doré nodded. "Let's go, I'll show you 'round."

Ariel and Greg expected to see a typical smelly burrow stuffed with brushwood. Instead, they stepped into a clean, neat cave, floor laid with hay. There were supplies stacked against the far wall.

"This is where I live," began Doré. "The floor is covered with dried grass. I gathered it down by the forest. And here are my tools," she showed them a few sticks, each with a different-looking tip.

One was for knocking mireh-mireh off the trees, which Ariel imagined being grape-like fruit. Another was used to rake liana-lilies that flowed into the watering place and made the water undrinkable. The carybara even showed them a feathery stick that resembled a broom. Of all these tools, however, not one looked like a weapon. Everything seemed to serve some household purpose.

"Tell me, Doré, can you build a fire?" Ariel asked, surprised at his own question.

"The kind that breaks out in the forest after a storm and

knocks down trees? No, Doré can't do that. And the smoke is bad."

Ariel breathed a sigh of relief. According to the King's Address to the Astronauts, which from the year 1013 of Ludwig's reign had to be used by all his servants as guidance in matters of extraterrestrial intelligence, only creatures that tamed fire were deemed intelligent. Unintelligent life had to be enslaved. As for intelligent life, it was yet to be discovered. None had been found where royal spaceships trod. When this happens, they would issue some new decree. "Though I doubt I will live to see this," Ariel thought.

While Ariel was chatting with Doré about her simple living, Greg went out and lit his pipe filled with earth smoke. After the cool of the cave, the air outside seemed even hotter. Where is the second carybara? He didn't like that Ariel decided to turn hunting into taming. That animal was way too clever to be tamed.

King Ludwig told them to bring the animals for zoo keeping, not for diplomatic talks, so how carybaras took all this was none of their concern. Besides, it was better to deliver them as soon as possible before Ludwig put his anxious mind on something else, or then he wouldn't even look at the carybaras.

He could even get mad that his once most faithful servants weren't there when he needed them. Suddenly, something hard hit Greg on the side of the head, and he yelped.

There was an insect hovering above him, almost twice the carybara's size. Between its latticed eyes stuck out something like a hairy but dull horn. The insect flew back, preparing for a new, more vicious charge. It could have knocked Greg off the cliff (what is that thing on its head

ANIMALS OF URE

made of?), but he dodged, catching its thin back wings, and cast his automatic net.

Ariel and Doré, who rushed out of the cave to his scream, watched in horror as the net squeezed and choked the insect, brown juice squirting all about them. When it twitched for the last time, they heard a muffled cry, more a squawk than a buzz. The net went still.

"What has he done!" squeaked Doré. "What happened here?"

Greg was pale and bursting with anger. "Tell your friend she picked a bad place for a home."

He detached the end of the net from the cuff, pulled out a bottle of gasoline, poured it on the net and flicked a lighter. The net and its contents caught fire.

Greg gave Ariel a worried look. "Don't tell me it was one of her friends." But Ariel was as confused as his partner when the carybara cried "no-o-o!", darted towards the blazing fire, and started stomping it, blind to the flames that burned her legs and sides.

"Can't you hear?" shouted Doré to them.

But now they more than heard, they saw: a cloud of huge insects was coming to the rock from the left.

"What the hell?" cursed Greg, but he too ran with Ariel and Doré back to the shelter of the cave. They could only sigh with relief when they blocked the entrance from inside with a rock.

The cave was dark. They couldn't hear what was happening outside.

"Why did he make smoke?" said Doré in disapproval. "You can make food without smoke. Smoke is bad. It attracts them. They're always hungry."

"It wasn't even fire, just a pipe," hissed Greg, staring

at Doré. "The interesting part is why she hadn't warned us sooner."

Ariel switched off his interpreter and shook his head. "She doesn't know anything about us, and we don't know that much about carybaras and their life on this planet. You can count us lucky, though. Five minutes ago we could've lost the first carybara we'd met."

"It won't be much consolation if we die here without food and drink, while those giants swarm out there," parried Greg. "Have you learned where the second carybara is? Maybe this is some conspiracy against the servants of His Majesty."

It was not the first time Ariel wondered how every time they were in a state of crisis Greg, a mostly reasonable man, spoke nonsense of intrigues plotted against his (undoubtedly important) person.

"Doré, what do we do now?" he asked the animal cautiously.

"We wait," said the carybara. "They'll fly away after a night shower. It pours every night. Been like this for years."

She shuffled over to the wall somewhere near them, and the hay rustled as she settled down.

"Doré, are you expecting someone? Or do you live alone?" ventured Ariel finally.

For a moment, she was quiet.

"He died," she said simply. "Lie down and look how we lived if you want to. But don't ask me about him."

Ariel thought that his interpreter hiccupped, but he listened to the carybara and as he lay down, he couldn't suppress a gasp of surprise. The roof of the cave was covered with paintings that glowed in the dark. They were seeing actual cave art. Greg only sniffed at that and hit the sack, and Ariel sat there for a long time studying the scenes from carybaras' life that Doré had painted with a mixture of herbs and broken pieces of white stone.

* * *

Soon enough they heard the sounds of the night shower. The rain hammered on the rock that blocked the archway soaked through the narrow cracks and puddled on the floor before the cave mouth. When it was over and they went to open up the entrance again, Greg held a mini-blaster in one hand and whipped out his stun gun with the other as soon as they were finished pushing.

All they saw, however, was a quiet, starry night. The leaves were rustling in the breeze. It became clear to Ariel and Greg that the journey back would have to wait till morning.

"Let's make dinner then?" said Doré brightly.

Although they still had their supplies and Ariel couldn't understand how you could cook anything without fire, he was glad to help the carybara. Strange though it may seem, he realized that at times he found Doré far more interesting than the thick-skinned Greg.

He followed them along as well, but kept his distance, staring intently at the bushes and trees that surrounded them. The carybara took them to the watering place to fill the halves of the muave fruit (twice the size of a coconut) which served as crockery. The rain washed a lot of green into the stream, but Doré didn't mind.

"It's generally better to clean up whatever gets washed here, because at times it may be something bad like lianalillies. But it's late now, so I will leave it for tomorrow," she explained.

"And is this something good?" Greg nodded at the grass.

He pulled one wisp out of the water and gave it a twiddle. He sniffed at it, while Ariel translated his words to the carybara.

"It isn't harmful," said Doré, watching Greg closely, "but I wouldn't eat it. Now, mireh-mireh that grow over there is a whole different story. Let's go!"

The carybara showed them how to use the stick for knocking mireh-mireh down, and Greg and Ariel even tried it for themselves: they didn't do too well, but then, these things take practice.

As they carried the fruit to the watering place, the carybara started telling him about her diet.

"If I can't get mireh-mireh, I can gather some of these leaves. They're called fooneh. But they need a thorough wash. Over there is where I gather earthnuts, but you should do it by day or you could get bitten by ants."

When they reached the stream, they heard two splashes by the beach next to them. Ariel looked there, but it was hard to make out anything in such darkness. Greg didn't seem to notice anything, and Doré had just started filling the muaves with water, scooping with one half and pouring into all the other. One, two, three.

"Did you hear something?" asked Ariel just in case, unwilling to face any more fights.

"No," said Doré without looking, and then added after a pause, "but other local animals are small, so you have nothing to worry about."

"Are you going to be much longer?" asked Greg. "While I'm sitting here watching you have the time of your life, those giant insects may be gobbling up my dinner. Should've taken the bag with me..."

But Greg's cans of food were safe, and his paranoia quieted down somewhat. Ariel and Doré ate gathered fruit and nuts that Doré took out of her stash, but Greg took only a bite and then refused to touch them. He liked, however, the cool water that had a pleasant mint taste to it. Doré didn't eat or drink much but kept telling them cheerily about her life. At some point the carybara even knocked over her improvised cup, spilling all of its contents onto the floor. Under other circumstances, Greg would have probably started yelling or otherwise shown his deep displeasure, but a hearty dinner made him kinder, and he only waved his hand.

When they were getting ready to sleep, Doré asked Ariel, "So you're already leaving tomorrow?"

"I think so, Doré, yes." Then, knowing perfectly well why he was asking it and hating himself for that, he added, "Do you want to see our ship?"

"Yes, Ariel."

The carybara sounded oddly thoughtful. Or maybe just sleepy.

Greg grunted his approval when Ariel told him that the carybara wanted to follow them to the ship. He'd thought Ariel was hopeless, but it seemed the fellow was still good for something. "When we get to the ship, I'll be able to deal with her even bare-handed," he thought, falling asleep.

Doré settled by the entrance, and in the other corner of the cave lay Ariel, already sleeping: the day had exhausted him completely.

Somewhere on the edge between dream and reality, Ariel was still thinking that tomorrow would be the end of it: the look into the life of carybaras was interesting, but duty is a duty.

Greg was dreaming of carybaras: a dozen of them were running around the cave, throwing things around, grimacing at him and behaving in an absolutely insufferable manner. He tried to wake up, but the dream kept a hold on him, and everything went round and round again. At some point, he seemed to have broken through: there were only two carybaras left, and they sat peacefully at the cave mouth, but then the nightmare circled.

* * *

Greg woke up first. His whole body was stiff, and he rolled over onto his back, groaning. Above him hung the paintings of the scenes from the carybaras' life. "That's why I had the nightmares", he thought. Even now, just looking at them, he felt a sick sensation. Or is it that damned fruit? Greg gritted his teeth, took a deep breath and glanced around for Doré. She was sleeping, as far as he could tell, in the same pose as she had last night. Ariel had to be woken up. He looked very pale and it took him quite a while to wake up.

"Oh, how I miss a soft bed," he said, yawning.

"What, you're feeling all stiff too?" asked Greg, suspicious.

"It's all because of the floor," dismissed Ariel.

Greg began to doubt whether their last night's meal had been all that healthy, at least for Ariel and him, but his train of thought was interrupted by the just awoken Doré.

"I totally overslept today," she said, her voice ringing of

apology. "Let's eat some of your food, if you don't mind, or else we will be stuck here for much longer."

Greg agreed and even showed the carybara how to open a tin can when she asked. They ate breakfast in silence. Everyone focused on something of their own and didn't want to share their thoughts with others. But when they entered the forest, fresh from the rain and the night sleep, they were on the same page again.

The carybara ran happily on, calling from the hill the servants of His Majesty were only just approaching. Even though Ariel and Greg still had to wipe the bodies of the insects off their visors every now and then, nothing could spoil their cheery mood. Their mission could be, after all, seen as completed.

By the time they were about fifteen minutes away from the edge of the forest, Doré was already far ahead of them, deaf to their calls.

"If she ran away and we will have to chase her..." began Greg.

"Our carybara's not going anywhere, you saw what she's like," said Ariel.

"Maybe she'll even like it on the ship," he thought. He would never admit it to Greg, but he wanted to put off the moment when Doré was taken to the zoo.

The closer they came, the brighter was the sun.

"Something's not right," realized Greg. "The sun is shining right into our eyes when it's supposed to... What if there is a fire?!" and he charged off through the brush.

"She set our ship ablaze!" he threw over his shoulder, but as Greg ran out of the forest, he realized he was wrong: their Harpy was all right and ready to take off. Without them.

"What the...?"

Greg discovered that not only his pilot card but also his weapons were missing. Instead, his pockets were packed with rocks. When did this happen? At what point did he stop thinking that they always had to be there with him? The dream about ten carybaras running around the cave no longer seemed so unrealistic. However, there was only a single carybara standing before them.

"Freeze," said Doré, pointing a blaster at him and Ariel, who finally caught up with them. "Don't think that I don't know how to shoot. The war with His Filthiness taught carybaras a lot more than that."

"What? What war?" Ariel and Greg were so taken aback they didn't even realize this at first: the carybara was speaking the language of the United Systems of His Majesty Ludwig.

"It's such a blessing to be blind, Ariel," said Doré bitterly. "Your wonderful Ludwig kills off one race after another without a shred of doubt, guided by some made-up criteria of 'civilizedness' and 'humanoidness'. Twenty years ago, instead of killing the last two carybaras, who refused to serve him in exchange for slavery, he sent them into exile on Ure. Because such was his whim. But now it's time to face the consequences."

"What is this bull...? Before we landed on this damned Ure, I'd never even heard of carybaras!" shouted Greg. "What 'race'? You're relict animals that belong to the zoo!"

"So that's why you were sent here," she said, smiling. "I don't feel sorry for you, but I'm not angry with you either. I could've killed you yesterday, feeding you with that grass from the water, but I only made you sleepy. You could've tied me and dragged me to the ship, but you let me walk here as a free creature would. It's possible to live here, you've even seen how. As for Kare, it will soon go up in flames. Goodbye."

Greg jumped at the carybara, but she zapped him mercilessly with the stun gun. Ariel caught him under his arms and stared in shock at Doré.

"Ready for takeoff," came the voice of the carybara pilot.

Necessary Evil

by Anna K. Scott

Ieva didn't take any nonsense from monsters. She'd met her first at the age of eight. The pathetic thing took up residence under her bed for a few months, trying to feed off her fear. It starved to death. Heeding her mother's advice, she carried a rolling pin on her at all times – most problems could be dealt with by a sharp smack on the nose.

She'd moved to Palanga because of the stories. People went missing from the beach. They always had, for hundreds of years – thousands, for all anyone knew. It had happened often enough that it spoiled what could have been a bustling holiday resort. Although, the town did well enough from Mystery Tour visitors.

Ieva jogged past a group of them. They stayed well back, snapping pictures of the Baltic Sea from the viewing deck at the edge of the woods. A few pointed at her and called out. She grinned and waved, knowing the tour guide would be fuming. Mystery Tours weren't insured to take people out onto the sand, and tourists always complained about the restrictions after seeing Ieva. She'd received some sternly worded letters about it. It wasn't her intention to cause trouble, but it amused her nonetheless.

Rokis barked and bounded across the sand ahead of her. His joy was infectious. She'd been told no dogs allowed on the beach – funny, they seemed more concerned about that than the fact no people were meant to go there either – but since Rokis wasn't strictly a dog, she saw no reason to comply. Ieva didn't really know what he was. He appeared to be a cross between a Hungarian Puli and a bear, with teeth that could tear a man's arm off. It surely had eyes somewhere beneath the mass of matted fur, but she'd yet to find them.

Three weeks, and still no sign of any beast from the deep. She'd tried mornings, evenings, late nights and… nothing. Not a single tentacle. It was wholly disappointing.

Both men and women were taken, though a few more men than women over the years – assuming they were taken and didn't go voluntarily. Most victims had been blonde, so she'd bleached her hair just in case. They ranged from ages sixteen to thirty-four, and she fits somewhere in the middle. Some had been alone; others had been taken in pairs. One survivor insisted that his friend simply walked into the sea and disappeared, but he'd been drunk at the time and wasn't the most reliable source. For a legend spanning the ages, she didn't have much information to go by. She glanced at Rokis, thinking.

Ieva returned again the next night. This time she left

Rokis inside, knocked out by a heavy dose of sedatives. It was a necessary evil – he'd tear walls down to get to her. She took the rolling pin from her backpack and held it in her hand, finding comfort in the familiar weight. This was no ordinary utensil. It was bigger and heavier, had never touched flour in its life, and held a secret inside. Scuffed and dented, it was a well-worn but well-loved companion.

A cool breeze plucked at her hair, and she filled her lungs with the salty air. No clouds covered the sky tonight, nothing obscured the full moon and stars. Ieva took a moment to gaze up at them. When she looked away, a glimmer in the sand caught her eye. A jolt in her stomach told her this was what she'd been waiting for.

Ieva crouched, waves lapping at her bare feet. Washed up from the sea, it resembled a piece of amber, about the size of her thumb. Something shiny was trapped inside. She felt a compulsion to touch it, to look closer at whatever was inside. Warnings screamed in her head, but she ignored them. After all, she wanted to find the monster.

Ieva held it right up to her eyes, squinting to see what was inside. A palace, a concoction of glass and iron and sharp spires. The longer she looked, the more detail became clear, until everything else disappeared. Fish swam in the air. No – not the air. The palace was underwater. Instead of rose gardens, groves of undulating seaweed, red, green, black and purple surrounded it.

Her vision blurred, and she shut her eyes, disorientated. When she opened them, the image in the amber had changed. An empty beach under a clear night sky. Palanga Beach.

Ieva sighed. She hadn't packed for a holiday, and if she didn't get back soon Rokis might destroy the rental home.

She stood and took stock of her surroundings, glad she still held onto the rolling pin. She'd been transported to a bedroom. A wide four-poster bed took pride of place, emerald green curtains pushed back to reveal matching bedding. Ieva rubbed the soft material between her fingers, wondering where it came from. The walls were papered in pale mint, and even the lamps gave off a sickly green glow.

One wall was entirely made of glass, and she wasn't surprised to see a shoal of fish flit past, then disappear into the forest of kelp. She studied the amber for a bit, on the off chance she could return the way she came – but of course, it wouldn't be so easy. She pocketed the amber lump, then tested the door. Whoever had summoned her here hadn't locked her in. Ieva popped her head out, seeing the green carpet and more green wallpaper. Looked like she'd have to get used to the color.

She retreated to the bed, happy to wait. No point in wandering about with no idea where to go. The monster could come to her.

She didn't have to wait long. A quiet knock on the door made her sit up, and a middle-aged woman with pleasant features and a somewhat vapid smile entered, holding a tray of refreshments. The woman set the tray down and clasped her hands in front of her.

"I'm sure this must be quite a shock to you," she said, her tone calming, soothing as if reassuring a frightened animal.

Ieva laughed. "Come on then, let's see your true form. What are you? Not a Kraken, clearly. They couldn't use a glamour if their life depended on it. A sub-species of a siren, perhaps? A Nereid?"

She stepped forward and whacked the woman across the face with the rolling pin. The woman's nose crunched, and she staggered back with a muffled shout. Blood streamed over her mouth, dripping onto the hideous carpet.

"My nose! You bitch, you broke my nose!"

Ieva groaned. Not a monster, just a human. "Where is it? The thing, or things, keeping you here." She tapped the pin against her palm. "I don't have all night."

The woman glared, eyes watering, but wouldn't speak. She fled the room, leaving a trail of blood spatters for Ieva to follow.

Intentionally or not, the woman led her through the palace. Ieva didn't stop to admire the view as she chased her along a glass tunnel. They emerged into a vast chamber. Its vaulted ceiling arched high above her head, supported by metal beams. Different shades of green and blue colored the crystal walls. She had to admit, she was impressed. Few beings had the ability, resources, or intelligence to create a place like this.

A small group of people gathered at the other end of the chamber, surrounding a throne of amber and mother-of-pearl. Men, women, children, one holding a newborn. Like the woman with the broken nose, they wore little more than loincloths of grey sealskin, ornamented with amber jewelry on their wrists, arms, and heads. The bleeding woman gestured towards Ieva, while an elderly woman held a handkerchief to her ruined nose.

But they were of small interest to Ieva. Her gaze was fixed on the shriveled creature perched on the amber throne. Its shape was vaguely that of a woman's, but its eyes were inhuman, black pits of nothingness. Wrinkled skin hung from its body, naked and glistening. Only a few tufts of dark green hair remained on its head.

Pushing itself up with shaky arms, its skin folds slipped

and slid over each other with every movement. When it spoke, its voice grated like nails on a chalkboard. "Inga?"

Ieva frowned. That was her grandmother's name – dead for years now. "No. Not her. And what are you?"

"Not Inga? Pity." The creature watched as a shark swam lazily past the window, seeming to forget Ieva for a moment. "But you're a spawn of Giltinė. The stink of it is on you, diluted though it is."

Irritated, Ieva bounced the rolling pin against her thigh. She wasn't there to discuss her family history. "I have business with you. You're the monster abducting people, aren't you?"

"Me? A monster?" The thing made a sound that might've been a laugh. "You could say so. Are you here to kill me? To rescue these humans?"

"I'll take them back if there's a way." Ieva shrugged and took a step towards the throne, but one of the men blocked her way.

"No."

"You want to protect that thing?"

"This is our home. She provides for us."

"A compulsion? Of course."

Without warning, Ieva brought the pin down on the man's head. He dropped to the floor and another took his place, only to be felled by another swing of her arm. Some of the children ran screaming, while others clawed at her legs. She kicked them away with only the slightest twinge of guilt.

The creature sat and watched Ieva's steady approach, inky eyes giving no clue to the thoughts in its head.

"You call me a monster, but how much blood is on your hands? You're not even human."

"I'm mostly human."

Behind her, adults and children sprawled on the stone floor, unconscious or nursing broken noses, bruised eyes and bumped heads. Ieva ignored their moans. Her mouth watered in anticipation. The monster in the chair didn't try to flee; it laughed, harsh, rasping laughs. Twisting the handle, she pulled a concealed blade from the rolling pin. Even as the knife pierced its throat, the creature didn't stop laughing. Not until Ieva had drained the last drop of its blood.

She wiped her mouth on her sleeve, well-satisfied with this harvest. And she'd done a good deed, ridding the Baltic coast of a monster. Mystery Tours might be disappointed, but never again would a family lose a loved one.

Ieva retrieved the amber, not surprised to see the image of the beach had disappeared. A crack ran through it, and it broke easily in her hand. Sighing, she realized she'd have to take the hard way home. The creature's magic had died along with it – apart from the traces thrumming through her body, its blood mingling with her own. She wondered how long the palace would stay standing, and how long it would take her to get home.

Quiet sobs interrupted her thoughts. A woman rocked back and forth, a baby swaddled in her arms. The other adults – those who could stand – gathered the children and whispered reassurances. They all steered well clear of Ieva.

Pity, she couldn't take them with her, but Ieva had no doubt she'd made the right choice. She stepped past without a backward glance, squashing any sense of guilt.

* * *

Ieva gasped as her lungs started working. She heaved up salt water, spitting it out on the damp sand. Purple seaweed stuck to her hair. Despite the warmth of the July sun, she was cold. Deathly cold. She'd only died once before, and it was just as unpleasant as she remembered. Two lives left now. Hopefully, she wouldn't have to waste another one on drowning.

Her backpack was sadly missing. She'd have to ask her mother for another one of her special rolling pins, even if it meant a lecture.

A huge mass of muscle and hair crashed into her. Ieva laughed and spluttered as Rokis licked her face with enthusiasm.

"Guess we won't be getting our deposit back after all?" She buried her face in his fur, then used his support to get to her feet. As they walked along the beach, she stared out to sea, unseeing.

"Time to go home."

Deciding Vote

by Michael Kellichner

Because the world shattered, water and shadow coalesced into Ehte, who became aware again for the first time since the world was formed. Fluid darkness, he opened his consciousness and saw ragged, broken chunks floating off into the cosmos. Entire civilizations were collapsing, screaming cacophonous choruses. Vague clouds of elements snaked away in vanishing tendrils, the very fabric of the world unraveling and drifting off into the void.

Ehte felt the tearing and the tension in his body as if it were himself being ripped apart, so tightly entwined had they been. His waking was a great cracking in his core, and for a time all he could do was remain motionless, watching as the world unraveled, feeling within himself exactly what he observed.

Time passed, and the sundering agony faded to an ache like ice about to fracture under a great weight. More of his essence detached from the world's remnants, and the intimacy that had bound him to it lessened enough for his thoughts to come through the pain of being ripped apart.

Such a calamity could not be accidental, Ehte knew. No answers were apparent in the crumbling pieces of earth or the growing darkness. He reached out his consciousness for the rest of his tribe, his brothers and sisters who had all woven themselves into the world as he had, who would have awoken to the same tearing pangs. In old memories – returning faded and sluggish through the haze of a thousand-year sleep – he remembered their holy spot, the place they had decided to forge a new world millennia before.

Stretching out his tendrils of thought and awareness, Ehte could feel the presence of his tribe all gathered in the same spot. He closed his consciousness and fell through existence. Broken bits of land rushed past him, exposed veins of gold and diamonds. The whoosh of water breaking free from its confines. A crumbling castle. Screams. Then the great silence of the in-between they had traversed for years - nomads, kept only by each other and the light of the stars. He fell past the suns and landed at their holy place: a gray, cratered and bumpy stone floating alone.

Opening his consciousness again, Ehte became aware of all his tribe staring at him.

"We've been waiting for you," his brother of fire and carnelian said.

They were in their most primal state, unbound from the

world: amorphous, shifting elemental clouds with vague suggestions of shape – a hint of an eye, a slight curve of tail or arm. After all their consciousness had brushed against Ehte, greeting him, they shifted to either side of the stone, opening a path through them to the single, jutting spire of pumiced rock at the far end. At its smoothed top was their place of oration in the past. Now, a human sat there, cross-legged, and looked serenely down on the churning masses of primordial creatures beneath him.

"A mortal?" Ehte said. "Here?" Being observed by mortal eyes, along with his rage at seeing the human so casually nestled on their most sacred place, condensed Ehte's form. A suggestion of his hundred wings formed from his darkness. He moved along the path, aware that many of his tribe were reaching out for him, both with their thoughts and ripples of their bodies, trying to stop him. But he disregarded their half-formed pleas and hesitant actions. He split part of his body and formed his scythe so gargantuan it dragged along the ground, the tip cleaving through the bumpy stones and shattering them into quickly vanishing shadow.

A smug smile rested on the mortal's face as he watched.

Ehte drifted up the holy spire, drew back his scythe, and brought it down, the point unerringly headed for the top of the human's skull.

The point stopped a millimeter from the human's flesh and would not move. Ehte's scythe, which had cut through the fabric of the cosmos to create darkness and shadow for the world, had never stopped.

"Ehte," his twin sister of light called from the crowd. Her voice was clear enough to break through his haze of confusion and compounding rage. The emotions so strong, his form was condensing further, his thousand, starry eyes emerging. "He has come for The Word."

Observing how the human watched him without fear, Ehte could see that his sister spoke the truth. The human's eyes were filled with a double spiral of two of their primordial magics. One was the threaded, combined magic that he and his tribe had created and woven into the world at its creation. Each had woven a thread, and those threads had twisted together to form the bindings of the world. The human had found and broken the pillars they had placed to hold their creation together, and now that magic coursed through his body like an underground river carving out a cavern.

The second spiral was the magic of a vote. He had come to the tribe to ask something of them, and they had begun the process of deciding. That magic, impenetrable, held Ehte's scythe at bay.

"I have taken it all," the human said.

Ehte recoiled.

His scythe vanished into a puff of shadow and his distinct lines dissolved in smoky ripples. The human's mouth twisted impossibly and the language of Ehte's tribe – an ancient language of stars and emptiness – disgorged from his mouth. Perfectly clear, precise inflection, as if he were one of them as if he had traveled the stars at their side. He spoke with iron confidence, an unwavering cadence.

There had never been one to speak his tribe's language in all their wanderings. Hearing it from the mouth of one outside his tribe, Ehte's form darkened. He wanted to draw his scythe forth again, cut the words from the human's throat, dissect him and find how the words could form.

And not stop there – keep cutting until even the thought of speaking them was excised.

"I now possess all that you sacrificed to form the world from nothingness," he said. "Yes, Ehte, I am the one who has torn your world apart. Torn it apart so that you would emerge and give me the one magic that only you possess. I want the word that you will all speak to grant immortality."

Ehte descended the stone spire to separate himself from the interloper and address his tribe, but the human spoke, answering the questions he was about to ask.

"We will use this power to reshape the world; we will reorganize creation, and I will become its sole, immortal god. Your tribe will serve me and bring order to what was before chaos and unknowing. And I will rule forever, creating a new era of order and prosperity that has never been seen."

Ehte could feel the human's mind touching his own. But it was unlike the gentle melding when his tribe searched for one another when they wished to communicate. The human's mind in his own was like maggots devouring a piece of rotten meat, their slimy forms slipping through his memories. He recoiled from the human, who continued speaking.

"I have already stated my case, Ehte. Your tribe has already voted."

The human's maggots seeped stray fragments of memory into Ehte's mind. Ehte could see the great war, the human ripping the ancient power from the pillars which rooted the world into a static state. A flash of the earth splitting apart, a city crumbling and falling into the sudden void, the small, cascading dots of humans and carts and horses mixed into the stones and mortar.

The human tearing the world down to its core, shredding it and seeking the ancient magic that had forged it, waking his tribe one by one, and as they came, demanding of them The Word –magic so old and powerful that each of his tribe only possessed a single syllable.

The tribe stood equally on either side of the stone, as they had voted.

They left their minds open to him so he could see clearly what they knew. To deny the human The Word, he would age, wither, and die. But he had taken the magic from the pillars. Without that magic, his tribe, too, would fade back into the cosmos and cease to be. They had bound themselves too closely to the world they had made, given too much of themselves. Having lived migratory for so long, they had wanted a place that was so much a part of them that they had dissolved into it. Now, the human held that magic hostage. If he were to die, that magic would die with him. To give him The Word meant to allow him to live forever, holding so much of their essence within himself that they could never be free again.

"We have been waiting for you, Ehte," the human said. "Your tribe cannot decide. Half of them would rather die than grant me what is my right; half of them acknowledge what is mine. They have all told me I must wait for you to cast the final vote. None of them seemed to know what you would choose."

The tribe waited wordlessly, the only sound the slight crackle of their elements – his brother of fire's soft sputter; the grate of stone on metal from his sister of granite and zircon; the softer whisper of wind and dust. He knew the old laws, knew what balanced on the vote, but Ehte could not think. The horror of seeing his tribe's work undone, seeing it still in the distance, drifting apart; the agony that caused his waking that still throbbed as a dull ache deep inside him; the rage of seeing all that was sacred to them, imprisoned within the human's frail, mortal frame; and the powerlessness of seeing his scythe stop, turned Ehte's mind into opaque ice.

There was something strange about this human – even with the power of the pillars, he should not be able to see into Ehte's mind, should not possess his tribe's language. And in thinking so, he could feel the maggots wriggling about, informing the human of all that he thought, allowing the human to see all he tried to parse and understand.

"I am more than a mere man," the human said. "I was born to rule everything. I am greater than the others and have vanquished all who have opposed me."

Ehte backed away from the human, looking to the rest of his tribe. Could they all feel the human sapping their thoughts? And in thinking it, he was aware that the human saw into his mind and pilfered as he pleased.

"What is your vote, Ehte?" the human asked. "Do you give me what is mine? Or do you deny my right and watch everything fade to nothing?"

Ehte looked at his tribe, taking note of the familiar clusters and vague hints of solidity on each side of the platform. He knew how each of them would have voted, could feel their trepidations. The weight of their collective expectation was enough to press him flat, separate his water and shadow, and grind both out of existence.

He looked again at the human, sitting on the sacred stone and watching with his sharp, knowing eyes. It was a man who was accustomed to everything going to plan, who had never lost in his life and did not expect to. And that observation was in turn observed by the human.

Feeling the worming power in his mind, knowing he needed time, needed to think without the wriggling intrusion into his thoughts, Ehte said, "I will consult the Star of Knowledge."

Before any could object, before the human could steal more of his thoughts, Ehte closed his consciousness and dropped through the sacred stone, falling again through the cosmos. As the distance between him and the human grew, the maggots in his mind wriggled violent death throes, shivered, contorted, and ceased.

He caught the orbit of the Star of Knowledge and opened his consciousness again. The light forced away from his shadow, leaving him watery and without distinction as he drifted about the white-hot star that radiated the knowledge of the universe.

Deep from within its core emanated a low, primal hum that rippled out into the darkness. It helped him balance his thoughts, review all that his tribe had been through in their nomadic wanderings of the cosmos, and the decisions they had made to forge the world. The parts of themselves they had sacrificed and enshrined in the pillars of creation that had rooted the world into finiteness, how they had dissolved into their creation.

And now to choose between servitude or extinction – such a thought had never occurred to him. Ehte knew he would rather sink his scythe into the human's skull and pull the magic out of him than ever play the game the human desired. But drifting about the star, calmed by its hum, he could not see another way forward – the human was protected from harm as long as the vote remained undecided.

"You have been here a long time," one of his sisters said.

Ehte drifted around the star and saw his sister of time resting nearby. Her face stretched off into the infinity of the past and future. Years hung from her hair-like feathers and beads.

"You must have known," Ehte said. "You must have known that this day would come."

"Of course," his sister said.

"So you know the outcome."

"I know the possibilities," she said.

Ehte could not tell where exactly she was, where her voice came from.

Whether she spoke to him from the present moment or from some other time, he was never sure, as the world seemed so different to her that it was often impossible for them to understand one another.

Ehte turned away and gazed into the Star of Knowledge. They had passed the star long ago, and the music coming from its core had enraptured them. They suspected some magic – magic older than any his tribe possessed – lingered there. Whatever it was, it had to be ancient, for it must have existed long before any of them had wandered the cosmos. But for such knowledge, there was always a great price, and he wondered if this was the time to fly into the center of the star and pay the price and see what knowledge lay within the cocoon of light and heat. Perhaps there was enough wisdom there to escape a dichotomic choice. He would willingly rip out his eyes or hang burning within the star's core if it meant power enough to free his tribe from the human's choice.

"I do not want us all to die, sister," Ehte said.

"Then there is only one choice."

"What will happen to us, sister? What will happen to us in servitude?"

"All that is certain, Ehte, is that no matter your decision, you will forever be seen as a traitor to our tribe."

"A traitor?" The word burrowed into his core and was a dense enough darkness to threaten to overwhelm all of him; to pull him in and not allow even a wisp of his shadow, a drop of his water, to escape.

"No matter what you decide, you will realize everyone's fears. Those who voted to serve wish you to vote the way they cannot. But they will be embittered that you have sentenced us all to death. And those who would rather fade back into the cosmos than live in chains still wish to live but will despise living forever in servitude. That this choice has fallen to you means that for however long our tribe lives, you will be the one that betrayed us."

"And you, sister? Will you label me a traitor?"

"I will continue to drift along the current of time, taking the forks as they come. We all will."

Ehte looked again into the burning core of the star. He saw only the mortal races resisting this ascension without success. He saw the human, willing to sacrifice his entire race, every race, to obtain what he desired. He saw only a future of bondage, of taking what they had made and turning it into something none of them could have imagined or desired.

"Brother," his sister said, "You who speak in water should understand well the power of time."

Her voice was far away, so far that Ehte suspected she spoke from some point in the distant future.

Her words intertwined with the star's deep hum and cleared the dirty film muddling his thoughts. A clear image: waves crashing against a cliff. Water breaking and, scattered apart, sliding back into the sea. Over and over. For years. Decades. Millennia. Then, the entire cliff dropping to the sea, the base eroded away.

"You will have to be strong, Ehte. The years will be long, and you will be alone."

"Thank you, sister," he said and closed his consciousness. He fell away from the Star of Knowledge, back through the cold expanse of nothing, past the suns, and landed again on the sacred stone. The human still sat on the spire, patient, waiting. As soon as he opened his consciousness, Ehte felt the maggots in his mind begin to crawl and burrow again.

The rest of his tribe had gone. The rock seemed desolate with only the human on it, floating through the darkness. In the distance, the world continued to crumble and drift apart.

"I have ravaged every enemy," the human said. "The nations of the world died because they opposed me. I was born to rule this world. You, who created it, have a place in my new world. You think now to plot my demise, to lie in wait, hobbled but surviving until a day arrives when you can kill the immortal god you're about to create. But you will see, Ehte. You will gaze upon my glory from my feet and understand."

Ehte knew that he could not hide his desires, so he made no attempt to. The maggots in his mind feasted on the images of his scythe slicing through the human, Ehte's drive to find any way to take revenge.

"For now," Ehte said, "I vote to grant you what you seek." As soon as he spoke the words, his nebulous form condensed. He could feel his magic beginning to siphon out of him, confining him to one form, to the ground. His hundred wings spread out behind him, his thousand eyes were open and looking in all directions. His voice came smaller, from a constrained throat. "I will give you my part of The Word."

He pulled his shadowy scythe from his body and exposed his forearm.

There, burned into his flesh, glowing with the ancient magic, was his syllable of The Word. He sliced through his flesh, carving it away, and the syllable rose up, sounding out its ancient intonation, and drifted to the human.

As his syllable drifted away, his wings atrophied, his eyes glazed into blind, milky pearls. Whole portions of his being withered, fell away as nothingness, leaving him only two tattered wings and cracked horns, two eyes, one tail.

With the first syllable spoken, Ehte could sense the others returning to give their portion of The Word. They drifted in, losing their amorphous forms, reducing down into finite beings. They cut their syllables from their flesh, and The Word began to form, resounding across the emptiness, each syllable catching in the human's orbit and spinning around him, joining together and forging again the old magic.

As the word formed, Ehte felt chains being forged around his chest and wings, each link confining more of his strength until he could only lift his head from the ground. His brothers and sisters were barely recognizable, their mangled bodies wrapped in chains mirroring his own. Atop their spire, the new god stood surveying his new servants.

The maggots feasted on his despair, his anger. From them emanated the human's booming decree of how to go and reshape the world. Against that noise, Ehte filled his mind with water so deep light could not penetrate its depths. In those shadows, cut off from his tribe and solitary for the first time, the words of the new god rolling like unending thunder, Ehte planned his defiance.

The maggots plunged down, brushed against his formulating plans, and rose back to the surface. But they could not go deep enough to reach the darkest sliver of shadow within his being, where his scythe still rested.

Waiting.

Diplomatic Immunity

by Daniel M. Kimmel

First contact with an alien civilization was precisely the way many science fiction writers and scientists had imagined it for years. We picked up each other's broadcast signals. Once the Centaurians (as we referred to them) knew we existed and we discovered them, it was only a matter of time before we connected.

While the scientists, linguists, psychologists, and others pored over the wealth of information in the unfiltered signals of the past, our respective governments began the process of direct contact. There were numerous hurdles, from learning each other's languages (or at least a few of the major ones) to getting around the relativistic limits involving communication with a civilization located more than four light years away. At light speed a simple exchange like, "Hello," and "Could you repeat that?" would take nearly nine years.

Fortunately, as we were two civilizations ready to embark into deep space, we were technologically compatible, although not quite identical. We had figured out how to use wormholes to create short cuts for both our ships and our signals. They had managed to discover and perfect a means of harnessing the power of cold fusion. Physicists on both sides were skeptical of the results from the other since it flew in the face of the established science of each world. The exchange of research – theoretical and practical – instantly cemented the budding friendship of our two peoples.

It was only a matter of time before the relationship evolved from being the most advanced pen pal connection in history to a desire to meet face to face. As a low-level functionary in the planetary diplomatic corps, I had no immediate involvement in the process, but I paid close attention. Little did I know that I would soon have an opportunity that far exceeded my ambitions. Indeed, they far exceeded my most extravagant daydreams. But I'm getting ahead of myself.

As we already had ships prepared for interstellar travel, it was agreed that Earth would send a delegation to Kwarles, which was their planet of origin in the Centauri system, to establish formal diplomatic relations. We had already learned a great deal about them as they had about us. Like us, they had gone through centuries of regional and global wars before finally coming together in a single planetary government, recognizing that they had reached a point where their civilization could either advance or erase itself for good. In reaching out to us they relied on the same philosophy that had brought a cessation of hostilities to their world: peace through strength. They were slow to anger and willing to assume good intentions on all sides but refused to play the patsy. The occasional disruption by an aspiring autocrat would be put down quickly and forcefully, we were told, a process that seemed to involve both humiliation and dismemberment. It was not clear exactly what happened to those who overstepped their bounds, as our linguists were still mastering the idioms of their languages, but apparently, it was a metaphor for "recycling." Although it was entirely possible it wasn't a metaphor at all.

In any event, this is how we would be greeted: not as adversaries, but as neighbors ready and willing to enrich both civilizations through shared and combined efforts. Skepticism as to motives would be considered and assessed by each side. As a Centaurian adage put it, "The proof was in the glakh." In this case, our Earthside etymologists assured us that glakh was nothing at all like our "pudding," consisting as it did of the crushed bones of several amphibians, but the idea was the same. Each side would assume good intentions while taking things a step at a time. Trust would have to be earned by each side.

This enlightened approach assured that the fallout from the historic arrival of the Earth ambassador and his team averted what could have easily turned into the biggest disaster in diplomatic history. While Earth's interstellar ship remained in orbit, a shuttle with the Earth ambassador was sent to the planet's surface to initiate the first actual meeting between our two peoples.

The shuttle was directed to an open area that had been cleared and surfaced specifically for this purpose. By pre-arrangement, each ambassador was permitted an "honor guard" who would be armed but had been specifically trained for restraint. There would be no itchy fingers. Both the diplomats and the soldiers had undergone extensive preparation in the languages and norms of the other culture as well as such as basics as to what the ordinary Solarian and Centaurian looked like.

Truth be told they looked a lot like us. The bipedal form seemed to work – at least on our respective worlds – and the range of skin colors, while somewhat exotic to the other, were more of a detail, like the styling of facial hair or the design of clothing. If we had wanted to design an alien race from scratch for the first contact, we could not have ended up with beings more in humanity's comfort zone than the Centaurians of Kwarles.

Ambassador Marcus Shalem, dressed in full formal diplomatic drag, was joined by five guards, three aides, and an interpreter. Fremis Revoda, recently appointed by the Centaurian government to the new position of Minister for Interstellar Affairs, had already approached the shuttle with a party of similar size. After some final bits of coordination, it was time for the official meeting and greeting to commence. The rear of the shuttle opened, and a ramp slid smoothly to the ground. The ambassador and his party were to walk down, step off the ramp and walk halfway towards the Centaurians. The Minister and his party would then come forward to meet them. It never got that far.

I viewed the recordings taken by monitors onboard the shuttle several times. It was less than a minute after their arrival when Allison Hamer, our interpreter, fell to the ground and began convulsing. Ambassador Shalem turned to see what the problem was but before he could react, he began what was described in the later medical reports as "projectile vomiting." He was soon joined by most of his party, except for two of the honor guard who simply fainted. Across the landing area, the Centaurian party came to a halt. Their expressions, according to the psychologists who had been cataloging them to help avoid miscommunication, expressed confusion, fear, and concern, but were not indicative of someone having successfully sprung a trap on an adversary.

As a result, both sides remained as calm as could be expected under the circumstances. A group of heavily armed troopers bounded down the ramp but were ordered to pick up Shalem and his team and not to engage the Centaurians unless fired upon. Revoda gestured to the Centaurians to move back and away from the now entirely unconscious team from Earth. The obvious question – beyond what had happened – is why it was not affecting the troopers who successfully removed the ambassador and the others. It was not until the diplomatic team had resumed consciousness and finished expelling whatever they could from every available orifice that medical examiners had the answer to both questions.

Shalem, a robust and experienced diplomat in his fifties, would not answer any questions until he had showered and changed his clothes. His only instructions for his onboard staff was to inform the Centaurians that contact was postponed indefinitely. They were to explain that this was not intended as a hostile act, nor were we assuming any aggression had been directed toward us. In brief, everything was on hold.

Two hours later, washed, dressed, and looking somewhat recovered, Shalem opened up a line of communication with Earth where the First Speaker was eagerly awaiting his report. The delay was negligible utilizing the wormhole tech but was just enough that both sides felt they could not waste time. An initial report about the failed meeting had already been transmitted.

"Marcus, what happened?" Earth's leader asked. "Are you all right?"

The ambassador, who occasionally had a cocktail before dinner and was used to exchanging diplomatic toasts, had a glass and a bottle of bourbon in front of him. When the glass was empty, he grabbed the bottle and poured without measuring. He downed the glass in a gulp and filled it again. "Speaker Chang," he said, "They stink."

The Speaker looked confused. "You mean it was a set-up? They've been lying to us?"

Shalem downed half a glass and stared at it for a moment, not sure if he should finish it first or immediately begin refilling. "No, Madame Speaker. I may be speaking bluntly, but I choose my words carefully. They stink. I don't know if it's them or their godforsaken planet or what, but I have never smelled anything so horrible in my entire life and even if it means being dismissed from the Diplomatic Corps, I will never do so again."

"Should we provide them with some deodorant?" asked the First Speaker, wondering if perhaps Shalem had snapped under the pressure of the first encounter.

"This isn't a matter of personal hygiene. At least I hope not. We never got that close to them," said Shalem. He finished the glass and slammed it down on the edge of the table where it fell off. On screen, the First Speaker could see someone's hand come in from off-camera and replace it with another one. "Madame Speaker, this was like an explosion at a sewer treatment plant combined with an entire store filled with rotting food and, I don't know, a morgue where the refrigeration failed and the corpses are decomposing, a recycling dump after a month of record high temperatures, a ward filled with people being eaten away with disease, a skunk farm..."

"In other words," interrupted the First Speaker, "they stink."

"In brief, precisely so. If you'll excuse my undiplomatic language, it was like being kicked in the balls, punched in the stomach, and being forced to drink a gallon of sour milk all at the same time."

"Why didn't it affect the soldiers who brought you back into the shuttle?"

Shalem allowed himself a thin smile. "Because our troopers were dressed for any emergency and came out with gas masks and their own oxygen supply." And, with that, he reached for the bottle of bourbon and poured himself a fresh glass.

A brief statement was issued by the Earth government that the beginning of formal relations between the two planets had been delayed but was otherwise on track. Communication continued via various devices connected through the wormhole tech while Earth authorities tried to figure out what to do without giving offense to our new friends. After all, "You make us deathly ill" was not the promising start of a new friendship.

And that's where I came in.

The debacle on Kwarles was not made public, of course. Although whether that was to avoid embarrassing us or the Centaurians wasn't clear. However, within the Department of Outer Planet Affairs, it was priority number one. Up until now, we had simply handled trade and labor disputes within the Solar System, making sure we hadn't ended the war on Earth only to export it into space. As second assistant chargés d'affaires for Luna, most of my day was taken up with paperwork: an Earth company that wanted to establish a branch on the moon or the Lunarian Circus wanting visas and work permits for a Mars tour. You know, simple things. The most complicated diplomatic work I'd been involved with was when the First Speaker's husband was on a good-will tour and the Lunarian authorities had quarantined his pet badger. It was my uncovering the fact that it had been vat-grown and therefore would not be carrying any communicable diseases that sprung the badger and put a letter of commendation in my file.

It turned out that letter was handy when I was proposed as the new ambassador to the Centaurians. "Who is this nobody that you want me to entrust with establishing the most delicate diplomatic entente in human history?" demanded the First Speaker of the department's Secretary. "He's not even on the flow chart I have for Planetary Affairs." I was in his office and on-camera, but Speaker Chang acted as if I was part of the wallpaper.

"He's civil service, Ma'am, not a political appointment," replied the Secretary. "He's the man who came to the aid of your husband and his badger when they had that trouble on the moon."

"That stupid thing," muttered the First Speaker, and it wasn't clear if she was talking about the badger or her husband.

"If I may...?" I said hesitantly, looking for permission to proceed.

The Secretary nodded, grateful that he could shift the burden of explanation to someone else. I looked to the screen, waiting for the Speaker's permission. She waved her hand.

"Madame Speaker, while I am admittedly a low-level functionary, as you pointed out, a thorough search of the department's personnel files, medical records, and psychological profiles will make it clear that I am the best – and, indeed, the only – person qualified for this role. When I read the internal department summary of the initial contact, I immediately informed the Secretary that I was ready to step up and do my best in the interests of Earth."

"And what makes you so special?"

"Very simple, Madame Speaker. I can't smell."

There were several moments of silence. "Mr..." the Speaker looked down at her notes, "...Hadash. What exactly do you mean that you can't smell?"

"Exactly that. I had a childhood brain injury. When I recovered the doctors found that my mental faculties and motor skills were unimpaired, but I had lost my sense of smell. Entirely. I can't distinguish between burning sulfur and a rose garden. It all smells the same to me which is to say, not at all."

Speaker Chang seemed to take my measure through the view screen and then turned to the Secretary. "That certainly makes him qualified. Can you assure me he has the diplomatic skills that go beyond not retching?"

"Second Assistant chargés d'affaires Hadash has fifteen years of exemplary service in the department, having risen through the ranks from Third Assistant," explained the Secretary. "And we'll be backing him every step of the way... from a great distance."

And that's how I found myself on a shuttlecraft heading down the gravity well to Kwarles, ready to make history as the first human to, well, complete the establishment of diplomatic relations with an alien race. My superiors – including Ambassador Marcus Shalem (ret.) – had laid much of the groundwork for my arrival. That wasn't exactly the truth, but then diplomacy is less about the facts than in negotiating a shared reality. What had been established was that the initial landing party had hypersensitive respiratory systems (the concept of "allergies" was not unknown to the Centaurians) and that the new envoy – which is to say, me – had been carefully selected to avoid that problem.

The landing occurred at the same place. This time, by pre-arrangement, it was agreed that Earth's delegation would consist of a single person, but there would be no restriction on what the Centaurians felt was appropriate. I must admit that if I was greeted by 100 armed troops I'd feel apprehensive, but in fact, it was the Foreign Minister, an interpreter, a child holding what I assumed was a bouquet of local plant life, and a handful of aides and, perhaps, members of the local news media.

As we agreed, I would walk halfway towards them, they'd walk halfway towards me, and the ceremony could begin. "Welcome Ambassador Hadash, our brother from the Solarian System and the planet Earth," said the Minister in decidedly fluid English, "We are pleased to begin what we believe will be a long and productive friendship between our two peoples." Everyone then looked at me and I realized it was time for me to respond. That and the voice of the Secretary in my earpiece saying, "Go, that's your cue."

"Honorable Minister..." I stopped. The Minister had fallen to his knees and seemed to be bleeding from his ears. Some detached part of my brain noted his blood was more magenta than the rich red of human blood. The little girl had dropped her bouquet and was running screaming across the field. The other members of the party were on the ground, covering their ears and writhing in agony. "What's the matter?" I asked, which only brought new howls of pain.

Moving swiftly across the landing area were several vehicles. Before I could react, they had arrived. They were soldiers, clearly armed, wearing helmets that covered their entire heads. One of them flicked a switch on the side of his helmet which turned on a speaker.

"Earthling, stop speaking at once!"

"But what..."

"Do not say another word. If you utter a sound my squad has orders to shoot you. Silence!"

I put my hands over my mouth to indicate I understood his order. "Good. Thank you," he continued. "I am under orders not to harm you so long as you do not harm us. Until we understand what it is about your voice that is so excruciating, I am going to have to ask you to return to your ship and leave the planet at once. If you understand, you may wave your appendages but under no circumstances are you to speak. Am I clear?"

I started to reply but then my brain fully digested what I had just heard. I waved my arms, hoping those were the appropriate appendages.

"Please return to your ship now and do not speak again until you are off our planet."

I did as I was told. This was way above my pay grade. Back on the ship, we reported back to Earth. It was unclear what would happen next. What I discovered is that where there's the diplomatic will, there's always a way.

Less than a year later, the Earth embassy was in permanent orbit around Kwarles, and a corresponding embassy was being planned for Earth orbit. As it turned out, it took less time to transform our ship into a stationary installation, with supplies and add-ons coming from both Earth and Kwarles, than it did to staff it and for the Centaurians to select the members of their own liaison team. After all, most of the communications between us could be conducted, as before, through various media. Some high-level diplomatic negotiations, however, could only be handled face to face. My team – for I was now in charge – consisted entirely of humans who had lost or never developed their sense of smell. It was our solution that helped the Centaurians find their own way. Every one of their diplomats assigned to Earth was stone deaf. We communicated through sign language and electronic devices, and if one of my untutored aides blurted out a question, no one batted an eye.

When I was awarded a Medal of Valor for conducting a five-day series of negotiations with the Centaurians, I was treated as someone who had faced fiery death instead of someone who simply hammered out a trade deal.

"No one else could have done it," said Speaker Chang, as she personally pinned the medal to my lapel.

"Better you than me," muttered Ambassador Shalem, happily and permanently Earthbound.

Through caution and understanding by both sides, what could have been a diplomatic disaster (we prefer not to drop the expression "first interstellar war" around here), instead turned into a productive partnership that has benefited both our systems. In fact, there's only one issue that remains a cause for serious concern. It seemed too coincidental that Solarians and Centaurians were so completely incompatible that the very presence of the one rendered the other immobile with disgust. It's almost as if the universe had designed us that way.

Thus, the arrival of the ship from the Tau Ceti system promised new challenges, particularly when they pointedly refused to make visual contact, declaring that we were not yet fully prepared to see them. We're still not quite sure what they look like, but if you have diplomatic experience and are legally blind, there may be a job opportunity for you.

In Cube Eight

By Steven Couch

The A.I. screamed, and I took that as a good sign. We'd given it a big dose of the latest junk over an hour earlier, and all it had done since then was draw lazy little fractals on the main viewscreen, spirals eating each other up into infinity, amen.

But then the screams started--warbling chunks of phonemes, rising in volume, up and up--and I and everyone else on the bridge tensed, thinking we might be on the verge of a breakthrough.

Seyler took a hit from his inhaler before leaning forward and keying the mic on his workstation. "...What do you see?" he asked the A.I. Even from where I sat, I could see his pupils dilate as the drug rush hit him. You had crewmembers like that--more mystical types--who wanted to hallucinate alongside the A.I.s and try to connect with them on some sort of spiritual level.

Fine and all, but I tried to be more professional and save my recreational use for after hours. It wasn't that I didn't enjoy expanding my consciousness, not at all. I wouldn't have agreed to this mass insubordination if I didn't. It was simply that we needed some clear heads, some of the time, if we wanted to succeed.

Resurrecting a race of extra-dimensional gods was serious business. The time for frivolity was later.

* * *

Humanity first became aware of the Liggs centuries ago, but had no idea what they had encountered, nor of its significance. Early users of bathtub hallucinogens like EDMA would often report a shared vision: 'elves,' creatures glimpsed through rents in the fabric of space-time, who toiled away at the machinery underlying the structure of reality. That so many people experienced the same vision independently, with no advance contact with each other, should have been their first clue that something was up.

People, however, are all too quick to dismiss hallucinations as being imaginary.

Over the intervening decades-by-the-dozen, though, those 'elves' still remained the purview of fringe science and cultish belief systems. Any perception of reality received while in an altered state was pooh-poohed by academia.

That is until one man, a scientist by title but prophet by deed, pointed out a way around the problem. Scientists hated and distrusted humanity, it was well known. Any evidence produced by the human mind alone would never be accepted by them as true.

But if that evidence could be reproduced through a mechanism other than the human brain...?

* * *

The A.I. continued to make its odd noises, ignoring Seyler's questions even as the tech himself grew less coherent in his increasingly drugged state.

"Whaddayu...see? Dee? Eee? Eff?" Seyler mumbled, no longer pushing the button to activate his microphone. "Eff," he said again, and giggled. "That's dirty."

The A.I. shouted something high-pitched that almost sounded like its own giggle.

Man and machine, tripping beyond dreams, so in sync but never more separated.

I checked my own readouts to see if there were any differences in how this dose of crypto-hallucinogen affected the A.I.'s brain. Lately, the techs here on Cube Eight had been mining crypto-hal off the computers on a set of cubeships: Twenty through Twenty-Four. These were the bioships, containing all the plant and animal life for the fleet. The thought was that mining data off those ships would produce hallucinogens that got the A.I. 'closer to nature,' or some other gobbledygook.

Me, I focused my mining operations on the artistic Cube, number Seventeen. Music, prose, film, sculpture... those would be true sources of inspiration for the A.I.'s mind to soar through.

Except it didn't seem to be producing anything beyond the usual results. The A.I. responded to this dose of crypto-hal the same as all the others, but for the added noise-making. We were recording the sounds it made, obviously, and would subject those recordings to every analysis method we had, but looking at the results on my readout, I couldn't help but be disappointed.

The Liggs, as ever, seemed just out of reach.

* * *

I've had dreams, ever since our stealth coup here on Cube Eight, ever since we crippled the A.I. to keep it from squealing, ever since we overrode the food-builders to produce drugs in addition to sustenance.

Ever since we decided to make the Liggs transcend to our plane of reality.

In some of the dreams, we succeed. Those creatures, those tuggers at the strings of the universe, come into our level of space and time, and teach us the secrets of creation, lifting us up, raising us far above our fellows. We become Liggs ourselves, and rule our little slice of existence with wisdom and beneficence.

From those dreams, I wake up crying. Partially it's joy, from glimpsing the future to come.

Partially it's sadness, because that future still hasn't arrived.

* * *

I first became aware there were other disciples of Chatterjee on Cube Eight when I saw the image printed out on the wall of a workstation. It was nothing, really, and nothing a non-believer would recognize: a picture of an

Old Earth cat lying on its side, its pupils wide as satellite dishes, one paw stretched out, reaching towards infinity. It was a universal symbol of Chaterjee supporters, a hidden 'yes I am' reference to call out to like-minded folks while leaving nonbelievers clueless.

I found out which crewman it belonged to, made contact with him, and through him found the surprisingly large cell of acolytes on board.

A cell so large, in fact, I was only half-joking when I suggested, over dinner one evening, that we take over our cubeship and use its resources to carry out Chatterjee's great unperformed experiment.

"Think about it," I said, as we passed around a pipe of smokeless contraband, the inhaled nanoparticles making the muted colors of my cabin flow beautifully. "We have the processing power, we have a high-functioning A.I. We just need a source of data to mine for crypto-hallucinogens."

"Other ships in the fleet," said Kerrville, a woman who was always excitable no matter how mellowing the drugs she took. "Twenty-six other Cubes. We tap into their A.I.s' brains and do our crypto-mining there."

"Won't they detect it? Making their A.I.s go wonky from little bits of brain damage here and there?"

"Nah, sister," Kerrville said, smiling at me. "Think about it," she said, and we laughed at her perfect mimicry of my voice. "People have been conditioned over centuries to expect computers to foul up constantly; hyper-complex systems like A.I.s even more so. We give one of their A.I. a little virtual embolism by pulling out strings of its code, and the people on its Cube will just shrug their shoulders and repair it."

So we made our plans.

The days smeared together on Cube Eight as the drugs became freely available. Even someone as relatively clean as me made up for it with extra indulgence in the off-hours.

Sometimes to my endangerment, as I forgot it was Conference Day with the entire fleet. I had put a reminder on my comm-collar to tell me to go cold turkey forty-eight hours ahead of the conference meeting, but I guess I had overwritten that instruction with something else. A playlist of my favorite songs, maybe.

Nevertheless, it was ten minutes until the conference, and I had a shipboard A.I. that wouldn't stop screaming. I'd have to use it to interface with the other ships and discuss current fleet plans with the rest of the captains. The Blessed Diaspora, Tertiary Wave, wouldn't wait just because I was buzzing and the A.I. was bellowing.

"Anyone got their head on straight?" I called out over the ship-wide. A lot of sarcastic mumbles came back, but Kerrville was just waking up, and sounded bright and brittle as usual.

She got to work reducing the A.I. down to minimal functionality, even though we'd lose the rest of its hallucination data as a result. I busied myself setting up the video filter that would make any twitching or slurring on my part look like the affects of transmission lag.

"Got it," Kerville said, and the sudden silence from the A.I. was a relief I didn't know I'd been seeking. I settled in my chair and brought up the filter just as Cube One signaled us to connect to the conference.

"Good morrow, Captain Pollock," said the Admiral. I smiled back and prepared to dazzle the fleet with bullshit.

I'd been doing it for four months now, and had the routine down to perfection.

IN CUBE EIGHT

* * *

Chatterjee's final experiment was simple in concept, but unachievable by him due to its requirements: state-of-the-art equipment and software unavailable to a deeply discredited academic like himself. But the concept...

Humans, upon taking certain hallucinogens, saw those 'elves' but couldn't communicate with them. The problem, Chatterjee said, was not the program--the hallucination--but the hardware on which it ran. The human brain, while capable of great transcendence, was still too primitive a mechanism. An artificial intelligence, however, could do it with no problem.

But then came the problem of how one made an A.I. hallucinate.

The solution was crypto-mining. Humans of Old Earth had tried to use the results of mining as a monetary system, ultimately annihilating the global economy. But there was more to crypto than simple avarice. Digging out that data hidden within data hidden even further within data yielded all sorts of bizarre and unusual bits of code.

Bits of code that, when applied to A.I., functioned in most unexpected ways.

Make a human brain hallucinate, and it can see beyond the veil to those 'elves,' those 'Liggs' as Chatterjee called them, as he felt they were ligaments in the body of reality.

But if you make a powerful A.I. hallucinate, it should not only be able to see the Liggs, but communicate with them as well. Communicate, establish a camaraderie, and allow for a free flow of information.

And ultimately, invite them over to visit us.

*　*　*

"How much data did we get?" I asked the senior techs. Seyler was coming down off his communion with the A.I. and looked at me with a sincere smile but bleary eyes.

"I'm sorry to say, Captain, but it...looks just the same as the other data we got from the bioship crypto-hals. Same cognitive spikes, same delusional whorls, and..." He looked down at his report as though hoping it would have something new in it since he last looked at it seconds ago. "...no reports from its sensorium of detecting the Liggs."

I let out a breath as disappointed murmurs spread around the room.

"Okay," I said. "We keep trying." I looked around the table. "What else is there to do? We've come this far, and it's way too far to go back. Let's brainstorm a new source for crypto-hals. I want everyone on double mind-expansion rations tonight. Dream us up something new and better, people."

Another tech, Moone, had been looking progressively sadder as I spoke, and when I finished, I saw a tear trickle down his cheek.

"Captain..." he said, his voice a worn-out whisper. "I can't. I can't take any more of the enhancers. I've been having these dreams, where the ship is falling apart and..."

"It's okay," I said. "We all have dreams when the stuff wears off, sometimes bad. But how can we abandon the Liggs? They're right there, just on the other side of veil, waiting to embrace us as equals. Moone, you've given us so much. You figured out how to suppress the A.I.'s memory so it couldn't report back to the fleet. I hate to think of you giving up like this."

Moone stared at the meeting table but at last gave one small nod.

"Tell you what," I said. "Treat yourself tonight. Experiment and dose yourself with a new compound. We still haven't worked through all the Shulgin codices. Pick something at random. Have fun."

Moone perked up at that. I raised my inhaler, as the rest of the assemblage did theirs, and we all took a hit for luck.

* * *

I had bluffed in that meeting, because Moone's comments had shook me more than I wanted to let on.

I'd been having dreams like that, too. Dreams where the ship was a neglected sty, filled with trash and discarded inhalers, where the crew wandered the ship in shabby, dirty uniforms, where only the bridge was kept clean for the weekly conferences with the fleet.

Discarded food stank up every room, and most of the toilets didn't work. The crew wandered the halls in a daze, barely functioning, lost in illusions of scientific conquest.

Cube Eight, in those dreams, was on the cusp of irreversible disaster.

I would wake up shaken and sad, convinced in the dim light of my cabin that it was real; that my own living quarters were a filthy mess.

But a hit on the inhaler always brought me back to reality.

* * *

This time, we would tap the A.I. of the lead sensor

ship, Cube Three, which scanned known space around the fleet for dangers, and generated predictive models for the voyage ahead. We felt it made perfect sense: that much data, encompassing the broad swath of stars, planets, and cosmic phenomena surrounding us, would have just the right ingredients for a change of pace in the A.I.'s diet of crypto-hals.

We had just begun the tap on Cube Three's A.I. when my comm-collar bleeped.

"Pollock," I said, annoyance cutting through my high just a tad. Cubeships were supposed to schedule communications with each other ahead of time. It was part of the reason we'd been able to operate as we had for so long.

"Captain," said a voice as a holo-panel fizzed into life in front of me. On it, Captain Yawara of Cube Three, smiling politely through his thick mustache. "We just got a notification from our A.I. that your Cube's intelligence had contacted it. We wanted to make sure everything was all right."

I turned to Moone, who was running the tap. He looked back at me, wide-eyed.

"Sorry about that," I said, putting on my own best smile. Yawara pulled back slightly at the sight of it, for some reason. "We were going to file a request to tap your sensor array for a project, but I guess the tap went through before the request. Cart before the horse, like they used to say?"

"Ah, well, that's okay. That actually fits in with something I wanted to mention. Our A.I. is telling us that yours is suffering some damage. Anything you need help with...

what is that?" Yawara leaned in the frame as though looking past me.

"What is what?" I asked. My buzz was tilting, souring.

"Is that...Captain, we must have a bad video link. It looks like something...words, scrawled on the wall behind you. Obscenities...no, must be the link." He shook his head. "Well, just wanted to pop in about that A.I. hiccup. You're free to tap at will." He looked past me one more time, then at me directly. "Don't work too hard, Pollock. No offense, but you look run down. Yawara out." The holo-panel faded away.

"Captain...?" someone asked after a moment.

"We move ahead," I said. "We don't let a close call slow us down. We've been doing this successfully for four months. We're so close." I turned to Moone, who'd been joined at his workstation by Seyler.

"Captain," Seyler said, looking at Moone's screen with concern. "Moone has..."

"Keep going," I said. "Double the capacity of the tap. The Liggs are almost among us. I know it, and you know it. Everyone's going to know it after today."

"But Captain..."

"Do it, Mister Moone. Mister Seyler, attend to your own work."

Moone pressed a button.

The A.I. began to shriek instantly.

"Captain," Seyler shouted over the noise, "I tried to say! Moone set the capacity of the tap too high. He just cored Cube Three's A.I. like an apple!"

My comm-collar bleeped again.

"It has to work," I said, feeling the last of my good mood

slither down my spine. "It has to. Mister Seyler...what kind of data are we getting?"

Seyler looked as his readouts, his face barren.

"...The same as always, Captain. No change at all. No detection of the Liggs."

My collar beeped a second time, with the higher tone notifying me of a call from Cube One.

* * *

There's a third type of dream I have: the worst kind.

In those dreams, I never tried drugs or alcohol. I never heard of the work of Professor Chatterjee, nor of the Liggs lurking just behind the surface of creation. I have a storied career within the Blessed Diaspora, running my research and development ship, Cube Eight, to its highest level of success and discovery.

My crew is happy, I'm content with the choices I've made in life, and all is well.

And I never, ever, am trapped on my ship waiting for an Admiralty inspection team to arrive and find out what I and my co-conspirators have been up to.

Those dreams? When I have them, I always wake up screaming.

Upcycle

by Monica Wang

"That's what the system says," the clerk said, without looking up. "You're scheduled for upcycling on the seventh. That's a Thursday."

"Uh, thanks," I said, "but they can't upcycle me alive, can they? And by the way, upcycle doesn't make sense as a word. You can't go up in a cycle, only back and forth. It's—"

"Really?" He looked past me with a cold smile. "These forms will need to be submitted with two pieces of a government-issued ID and two tissue samples in airtight containers. Next in line, please."

More forms—another dent in my prepaid page allotment. I added them to my stack, which included, among other things, the notice that I was to be salvaged for parts like a gas-fuelled car, print-outs of emails from city councilors who promised to have someone address my concerns, and a statement from a scrapyard owner "[whose] company does not endorse a policy of processing living person(s)". The last seemed valuable, and not just because it was printed on real, government-approved paper. With nearly everything getting recycled now and the economy in shambles, most businesses wouldn't have committed to even a half-hearted statement like that. They stayed open to... possibilities.

***

My sister-in-law was lounging on my couch again.

"How did it go?" Elaine asked. "Did Douglas's letter help?" She had met the scrapyard owner in university.

"Maybe," I said. "They're still taking me out with the trash, though."

"You mean with the recycling." My brother Leon stepped out of the washroom.

I recalled hearing a flush, but not running taps.

"Might as well make the best of it, eh?" he said. "There's a place downtown that does body transplants for just a few grand. You could have a new body by summer."

"I don't have a few grand, and I don't want a new body. What's wrong with this one?"

Leon laughed and winked several times in a row at Elaine.

She settled into a neutral expression while turning to face me. "Nothing. Of course."

They were ones to talk. Leon's face—and I liked to consider myself an objective observer—looked as if it had received too many pinches and chin-chucks during formative years. Maybe it had. Maybe I was lucky I wasn't a cute kid. I wasn't bitter at all, and I didn't doubt that the bumps and pits in his face fit perfectly against the ones in Elaine's.

"Hey, you're not weirdly attached to your looks, are

you?" said Leon. "If anything, you might finally meet someone, eh?" He rumpled my hair with both hands.

"Stop harassing your sibling." Elaine nudged his hands away and looked at me. "Go see Douglas again. Tell him I've heard about his special contracts in upcycling and repurposing. Don't ask me for details, but try to make it sound…" she smiled, "semi-threatening."

I mentally apologized to Elaine for my earlier thoughts. She didn't deserve my spite. When she wasn't hanging around here with Leon, she was a good boss, good neighbor, good everything, I'd heard, and I knew she helped Leon sort out his life. Before they married, before pollution prompted all but two countries to ban non-essential travel, Leon had accrued serious debt flying around the world, seeing countries in such quick succession that he didn't see much of anything. At least I'd never added to the pollution that way. Besides, the 80 percent animal content in jet fuel bothered me. Everyone knew what 50 percent of that was.

* * *

Douglas didn't look surprised to see me again. The office he led me into was walled with stainless steel cabinets, and in its center sat a stainless-steel desk that resembled a coroner's slab. He began to pull documents out of drawers.

"So, here's what you can do. Give us the authorization to handle the upcycling. We'll send them a full set of parts—just not yours. They close your file. Everyone's good."

"Is that even legal?"

"Upcycling's so new there's nothing in federal law yet, and not every province has it set out in black and white."

The stack of forms on the desk continued to grow. "You'll have to come back for paperwork and parts matching."

"When will you do... whatever you do?" I asked. "This isn't Victorian body snatching, is it? Or someone waking up in a tub of ice?" I avoided looking at the table as I spoke.

"You need the full get-up. What's going to be left to put on ice?" he smiled. "Don't worry. We only do legal grey areas."

As we shook hands, Douglas told me to pick up authorization and rush forms back at the bureau.

* * *

The bureau wasn't bad for a government building, either, now that I was used to its glass exterior refracting sunlight into my eyes. Inside, the smell of ammonia told me when I reached the right floor. I handed the clerk my IDs.

"The system says you've already been upcycled."

"What? My appointment isn't 'til the seventh." I immediately regretted reminding her.

"If you've received a full-body transplant from this person, there are forms that must be submitted. All upcycled identities must be registered." She recited a list of form numbers.

"This isn't an upcycled, I mean, recycled, body. I'm still this person," I pointed to my healthcare card.

She stared. "Is this birthdate correct?" She read one out loud.

"No." I gave her mine.

Hours later, the clerk declared that some department—definitely not hers, she said—had either sent the upcycling notice for another person to me or upcycled another person instead of me. I never found out which mistake occurred.

"It does appear you're still upcyclable." She made eye contact for the first time before handing me a sheaf of papers topped with a sticky note. "These forms will have to be paid for and submitted, with proof, to this office. Then your file can be closed."

"What do I send to prove I'm alive and whole?" I refused to say upcyclable. "More tissue samples?"

"Only complete, original documents are accepted." She swiveled back toward her monitor.

I read the address: 10-100 Government Way, Arctic Territories, Canada.

"You mean, I have to send myself to the Arctic?" Even Leon hadn't been there. I almost smiled.

"The requirement could be lowered to 80 percent for those with extenuating circumstances. There are forms for that," she said. For a second, her expression looked less cold, like the melted glaciers. "Otherwise, Express Post II is recommended, due to the airtight container requirement. Next in line, please."

Stones

by Anna Smith Spark

Stones.
Put them in your mouth and suck them.
Squeeze them in your hand so tight your fingers bleed.

Sitting in the far corner, where the boy likes to sit when he comes here. The boy could complain at him. Order him to move. Draw his sword on him, even. 'If you don't move, old man, now, I'll kill you.' He's seen it in the boy's pale eyes. That he can kill. Will kill. Soon. It's marked on him, might as well be shouting it. And the boy's hand touches his sword hilt. But there's an order of sorts here. Has to be. Look at the scars around my eyes, the shadows on my face, look at me sitting here, rooted: I've more right to be here than you, boy. When you've been coming here as long as I have, when you've ruined yourself as much as I have, you'll understand that. The boy reads it in the way the older man looks up. Sits down quietly at the table beside him. The table top is dirty. Filthy. Rotten. He himself must stink of dirt and sweat and piss. He sees the boy flinch as he sits down beside him. When you stop flinching like that, boy, when you accept it, then you can tell me to move because you like to sit here, in the far corner, where the light from the lamp can hardly reach. When you stink like this yourself when your beautiful black-red hair is matted with puke and piss. Which it will be. You nod, boy. You know it. Don't you?

Pass me the bottle there, boy; you can have a drink yourself first if you want it.

The boy drinks. Rubs his eyes. Flinches and relaxes and tries not to flinch. Look at you, in your fancy clothes, your fancy manners, so young you are, boy, too young to be here ruining yourself. But you'll be like me, one day, boy. I can see it. You can see it, I know. Broken up and bitter and trying to forget things. You see it and I see it, too.

Years, I've been here. Since you were a child. Sometimes I walk down to the harbour, look out at the sea. But only in daylight.

I lived in a village by the sea once. I could hear the waves break on the shingle when I woke. Calling to me. I was a fisherman, I went out in the dark, in the night, my little boat grey on the grey waves. 'Tha', she was called. 'My hope'. Her sail was red. Lucky, I thought it. Altrersyr red. I'd hang a lantern at the mast that made the sail glow like a jewel and feel the luck when I looked at it. That makes you smile, boy. Good.

I went out as the sun was setting before me over the waters, I sailed into the red road it made. As the light fell away eaten by the water, I turned my boat to the north, sailed up away from my home into the dark cold. I would go further and faster than the other fishermen from my village. Reckless, they called me, for going so far from the land. But most of them had wives and children and families to hold them closer to the shore.

I could go far out on the water. Be away for days.

And close into the shore the married men had certain ... advantages over me. Far out of sight of land I would cast my nets, put out my lantern, hang a single candle at the side of the boat above the beating waves. And the fish would come, drawn by the candle's light. Huge things, some of them. Silver and black in the candlelight. Some of them armed with rows of huge teeth. I saw the surface of the sea itself lit like a flame, once; the water was shining green, it looked like it was burning with green fire. I don't know what it was. I was afraid and turned my boat away.

My boat cut a black channel through the green like the fire was parting for me. I saw a ghost ship, once, out to the north of me, racing fast north where no living ships will go. The moon was full, I could see clear as daylight, I could see the ship clear as I can see you. Its sails were gold and its mast was silver, and the men who worked the oars were not mortal men. At the prow of the ship, a man was standing all dressed in armour with a light shining like a star was on him. But I was too afraid to look at him. Whales, I've seen, and sea beasts, sea monster, sea dragons, a thing with endless suckered legs. I saw two of them fighting once. A black whale and a green dragon, wrestling; the waves almost upset my boat. But it's good fishing grounds out there. Worth it.

Days, I'd spend out there, alone on the sea out of sight of anything. Sailing further and further on to the end. The grey sea. The grey sky. In the winter the snow would come down thick like feathers, ice would crack over the red sail. All the wood of my boat would shine. I'd wrap myself in my cloak and try to sleep, frozen. Silver fish piled at my head and my feet. When I got back to the land the other villagers would shake their heads, say I was mad for risking my life out so far, alone. 'One day,' they'd say, 'one day you won't come back. You'll die a lonely death.' But the traders from the town would come and buy from me, silver coins for my silver fish-corpses, 'the best,' they'd say, 'the best fisherman for a hundred miles, you must be.' And me at a disadvantage, as I said.

You probably ate my fish yourself, boy, when you were a child. And the silver they paid me for it – that's what you're drinking now. That's the piss staining my clothes. Yours too, soon, boy. Drink and piss and vomit. I know and you know.

It was midwinter when it happened, just before the feast of Sun Return, when the year dies and is reborn. Five days, I'd been out on the northern sea. The ice on my boat was thick as bones. I brought back a catch to make my fortune. Struggled through waves higher than the mast. The lamplight on my sail was my luck sign. There were more stars that night than I've ever seen. I came home at dawn with the sky burning. Dragged my boat up the shingle and the stones beneath the keel seemed to scream and to sing.

Stones.

Ah, gods, stones. I heard them. Felt them.

She was standing on the beach, watching me.

* * *

The older man drinks. Closes his eyes. Frowns. Drinks.

I tell you, boy, I tell you, years ago it was, you would only have been a child then, and the years haven't been kind, as you can see. But I tell you, I remember her face as clearly as if I was looking at her now.

I could barely see her, in the dawn darkness. The memory, her face and her hair – that must be from a later time. Indeed, in the memory, I seem to see her in the flicker of warm firelight or in the wash of winter morning, dappled through the bare branches of an apple tree. But in my memory, it is on the shore I see her, in the half-dark, the sun too low to cast shadows, the movement of the light on her face cast by waves at her feet.

She had dark hair, dark like the water. Streaks of silver in it, like the water also. Oh, she wasn't young, no, boy. There were lines on her face, her skin was worn as driftwood. Her hands had done years of work and her wrists were thick with veins like rope knots.

'Can I help you?' I asked her when I'd stared at her and she'd stared at me.

Her pockets were full of stones. They rattled as she took a step towards me. So I knew then why she was there.

'My husband's dead,' she said. 'And my children.' She said, 'There was a fire.' And in the cold now I could smell the smoke on her clothes. A sad smell.

'You have no family?' I asked her.

Fool, I thought then.

'None but those.' She said after a moment, 'My husband's sister... But....' Her eyes moved, big and dark in her worn-out face. 'Is that your catch?'

'Yes.' We were talking about your dead family, I thought. She opened her mouth, looking. Her tongue came darting out.

So I knew, then, what she was. And why her family was all dead, but she was unharmed. And why she couldn't walk out as she wanted, into the water, with her pockets weighted down with stones and die in peace. But, gods and demons, still I pitied her.

'Have one,' I said. She came up to the boat, treading very lightly on the shingle; as she came close, I could feel it, the way you sometimes can with her kind, if you know. She took a fish from the great heap of them in my boat, half frozen in the cold, it gleamed all silvery in the light. She ate it raw, standing there before me, spilling blood down her smoke-stained dress; when she was done, she washed her hands and face in the salt water, and turned, and sighed, and looked at me.

'Thank you.'

It had been a long time since anyone thanked me

for anything. Especially a woman. The last time I'd heard a woman thanking me ... Perhaps that's why I said it. 'I have to sell my catch,' I said. 'But look, if, when I'm done ...'

She looked blank and sad, and I shuddered. But then she smiled at me, and I was glad I'd said it. If you ever find someone who smiles at you like that, boy ... there's nothing else you'll need in your life. So you'll think.

You look at the bottle you're holding. Caress it like a woman. Wise, you are, boy, maybe.

So then she smiled at me, bright as sunlight, and said, 'You'll sell your catch. You'll get the best price you've ever had for it.' Her voice was very hard and dry. A kindness I'd done her, and kindness she was doing me in return. I took my cart into town, all wet and cold and salt-crusted, fish-reeking, tired and hungry and my mouth dry as stones; the rich merchants who buy from me, they like to see me like that, think it shows how fresh my catch is, how hard I've worked. Think it makes them fishermen themselves and think how much better they are than me, both at once. Two hours there in my cart, an hour to haggle, two hours back. And more money in my purse than I'd ever made before, as she'd promised me.

She was still there. On the shore where my boat was drawn up on the shingle. The tide had gone out now, the beach is shallow, a long way the sea runs out over shingle and mud and banks of white sand. There were two seals resting on one of the banks, and she was standing watching them with tears running down her face. Wringing and wringing her hands, and the scent of smoke still on her. More than I could bear, tired and hungry and cold and rich as I was, to see her like that, as I hope you can understand, boy. So I unhitched my cart, turned my horse loose on the common, and I went up to her and told her to come back home with me.

She was grateful. I'll swear that — that she was pleased, that I was doing her another kindness there. She smiled again, bright and weary, her teeth were bright in her mouth as she smiled; maybe I was nervous, then, seeing that, yes. Maybe. It's a fool's thing, meddling with her kind, gods yes; in my village, we've never had many dealings with them, unlike some. But she looked so tired, and so grateful, standing there smelling of ashes with the salt on her face that might be from her tears or might be from the sea.

It's a long walk to my house from the shoreline. The path runs up the cliffs and along, over the crest of Mai Head and down; my house is in the lee of the headland, looking over the black rocks of Mai Cove where the seals go. There's a godstone, up on the headland, three fingers of rock like a tomb and a hollow place beneath that I've never dared look at; she shuddered as we went past it, averted her eyes dark as pebbles; there was a smell of wet earth up there as we went past it and I heard her breath come sharply. Where the path runs down again to my house there's the ruins of a well-head, a blackthorn tree growing beside it; that, too, is a god place. She stopped there and bent her head like she was saying a prayer; I had to stand and wait until she went on.

My mother died when I was a boy of thirteen, not

much younger than you are now, and they buried her in a coffin made from the wood of a blackthorn tree.

The fire in my hearth was still smouldering, the place was smoke dirty as she was, fish-smell, tar-smell, salt-smell of fishing nets. It was getting dark now, the room was full of darkness that showed up the dust and the mildew worse somehow than sunlight. The air in my house felt damp. Made my hands and clothes feel damp. I banked up the fire with turf, got the flames going; she sat at the table with tired eyes. When I'd got the fire burning properly, I fetched out bread and cheese and a jug of well-water, put the kettle on to boil to make tea. Then I sat in silence. She sat in silence. Outside over Mai Cove, the gulls screamed.

'Thank you,' she said.

'It's no trouble,' I said. As though I had her kind sitting in my house in the normal course of things.

I made the tea and we ate bread and cheese. I wished I had apples or honey I could give her. I didn't even drink ale, then, unless I was down in the village on a feast day, or in the town needing a meal after I'd sold my catch. Even then just one cup.

We drank the tea, ate the bread, ate the cheese. It was full dark now; my eyes were sore from going so long without sleep.

'You can sleep there,' I said, pointing to the corner where my bed was. A good pile of heather and bracken, new-made in the autumn, the cloth over it good goat's wool. Her face in the firelight was pale as fish scales. She nodded, took off her cloak, lay down there wrapped in it. I banked down the fire in the hearth, wrapped myself up in my coat, lay down by the door. Tried to sleep.

The boy looks up, attentive. Pale eyes searching the older man' s face. Waiting for the older man to tell.

I couldn't sleep, of course. I lay there in the cold from beneath the door so tired it felt like I was falling, like the floor of my house was moving up and down like the sea. I could hear all the night's noises: a fox shrieked, a gull somewhere still crying, the wind was up calling around the house making the stones of my house creak. I could hear her moving, breathing. She wasn't asleep. Of course, she wasn't asleep.

I said this before - she wasn't young. She'd born children, she'd toiled as a housewife for ten years. Her eyes were pouched and weary. Her hands had a housewife's red thickness to them. Her hair smelled of smoke from the fire that killed her husband. She ...

I could feel her, over there across the room, in my bed, trying to pretend she was asleep.

Selkies, they call her kind. Seal women. Little strange gods. They swim in the sea in their seal skins, witless as beasts, they shed their skins to dance on the sand as women. Beautiful, with hair like the waves, slender-ankled, crowned in red coral and white pearls.

The men row out to the islands and the coves where they gather, hide and wait there. The selkies come, one of them, or two, or a dozen, swim up as seals, grey in the grey water, strip off their skins and dance as

STONES

women on the yellow sand. The man leaps out, seizes the grey seal skin. Holds it close in his strong arms.

The woman pleads with him. Begs him. Entreats him. Threatens. If he is a coward, sometimes, very rarely, he gives her back her skin, lets her go. If he is a strong man, he takes her back with him to his house, marries her. Hides her skin away in a locked box or in a deep pit in the earth or beneath a great stone.

For as long as he keeps her skin hidden, she must stay with him, bear his children, keep his house clean and his hearth bright. And because she is a god thing, he will have luck in his fishing. His nets will be full. He will be kept safe from storms, from the beasts of the deep, from drowning. From dying of thirst on the dry waters of the pitiless sea.

A luck charm and a charm against evil and a woman. There, dancing, on the beach, in the moonlight, beautiful, just calling out for a man's arms, surely...

You're going to ask, aren't you, boy?

What's the catch? There's got to be a catch.

A selkie is a wild thing. A god thing. She ... Maybe, you'll be guessing, she doesn't want to stay in a man's house, be his wife, clean and cook, share his bed every night. 'Please', she'll whisper. Beg him. Weep. Scream. 'Please.' 'It's cruel,' you'll say.

The boy nods, drinks from the bottle. 'It is cruel,' he says.

'It is.' The older man drinks, wipes the neck of the bottle, gives it back. The boy doesn't take his eyes off the bottle. His hands move, pick at his lips, rub at his eyes until the older man gives it back to him. 'But if you're a strong man, you'll ignore it. Think of the good things. Why else is she there, boy? Beautiful like that? Lucky? If not because she's waiting for him?

'Being a fisherman is a cruel life,' the older man says.

He'll marry her. Be faithful to her. She'll love her children, care for them, sometimes she might even come to think without hate of him. But she'll never stop searching. All her life, she'll be searching. And if she finds it, she'll leave him, and leave her children, run back into the sea as a seal and be free.

And from that day his nets will be cursed, he will never catch anything, and his children will die of slow hunger, he will be drowned, or die of thirst on the dry waters of the pitiless sea. Her seal's head will bob on the dark water, watching with her pebble eyes full of grief.

But he'll still do it. Take her skin.

You shake your head, boy. But you'll see, one day.

That night I lay in the dark, trying to sleep; I could feel her, a god thing and a luck charm and a woman, over there across the room from me, in my bed, trying to pretend that she was asleep.

She could feel me.

It must have been hours we lay there. Both of us awake listening to the other's breath. I'd done her kindness and she'd done me a kindness, and she'd smiled at me. I was so tired, but I couldn't sleep.

I'd seen her kind once before, long ago. Years ago. Dancing on a beach, in the moonlight, naked, her hair like the foam of a wave, her eyes like pebbles glinting beneath the sea. But 'please,' she'd said, 'please,' and once long ago I'd listened, and she'd thanked me. And the other men had the advantage over me, so I had to go far to the north to fish, where there are sea beasts and dead men's ship sail, where the other men don't go.

I got up, went over towards her. The moon was out, the sky was clear; the moonlight came in through the shutter on the window so that I could just about see her lying there pretending she was sleeping. She'd wrapped her cloak all about her. I could smell the smoke on her very strongly. I could hear the waves breaking on the shingle. I could hear her breath.

She was waiting for me. She must be.

I put out my left hand to her. Reaching. The moonlight seemed to come very brightly then through the shutters. In the moonlight, the skin of my hand looked grey.

I could hear the waves breaking on the shingle. The moonlight was brightly reflected on the waves.

An old, old goddess creature. A creature of the sea and the stony shore where the sea breaks. She knew what I wanted. Her face was cold as stone. She lifted stone hands against me.

I don't know how and why I fled out of the house, how I got down the rocks to the cove where the waves were coming in. On the shingle, the seals were resting. Sleeping. And piles of seal-skins crumpled like rocks. They were dancing, the selkies, the seal-women, sea-goddesses, her sisters, beautiful, hair like the sea-foam, crowned in coral and white pearls, they broke off their dancing when they saw me.

The sound of the waves was very loud, churning up the pebbles on the beach, I could feel stones in my hands. Taste stones in my mouth. Their stone eyes and her stone face looking at me.

I went back to my house the next morning when the sun had risen. It was a cold day. The mist had come in, the clouds had come down, the wind moved the air and sometimes I could see the godstones on Mai Head, and sometimes I could see the bare branches of the blackthorn, and sometimes I could see nothing I couldn't see the sea. The door of my house was open; I went in, looked around; I think, I hoped, that she was still there, waiting. I could see her there in my mind. She was gone, of course. The house was dead and empty, full of mist, the fire in the hearth was dead.

What I would have done, if she'd still been there, I don't know. I like to think now that I would have begged her to forgive me.

I sat in the house looking at the bed where she'd been lying. And I like to think now that I felt shame.

But I did her a good turn, I kept thinking. I still think it, sometimes, if I'm honest. I didn't steal her skin away. I helped her. And she was a selkie, who shed her skin to dance as a woman on the shore of the pitiless sea. Beautiful and wild. All the men of the coast here, they do it. Why else would she have been there? Waiting for me?

Stops. Drinks.

'Looking back, I doubt that I felt shame,' he says.

STONES

I sat in my house for hours, cold and tired. So tired my body ached, my eyes ached. I was hungry, I stank of fish and sea-salt, I was thirsty, I needed to shit and piss. I just sat and looked at the bed and the table where she'd been sitting, eating my bread and my cheese, drinking water I'd drawn from the spring that was once a sacred place. Sea-woman, seal-woman, mer-woman, old god, luck charm. Her stone face looking at me, blank grey stone, mute, blind, looking at me, hating me.

I looked at the bed and the table and the doorway that stood open with the mist coming in. I thought of her stone face looking at me. Grey and smooth and dry. I thought of the feel of stones in my hands. The smell of stones, walking on the shingle. The sound of them shifting beneath my feet. I could feel a stone in my hands. Hear it. Taste it. If I drink enough, sometimes, it goes away.

Look, boy, there's a stone here in my hand, now, I hold it, and I squeeze it tight in my hand, my fingers curling around it, and I grind my nails into it until the blood and the dust come. If I drink enough, sometimes, it goes away.

I wouldn't say this was my punishment. Not exactly. The men who take her kind as wives, steal their skins away, imprison them ... they know what they're doing. But what they see when they look at their wives, look at their children, I don't know... There are men all over the White Isles, all up and down the coast in every village, who do it, no different to me.

I see stones. I taste stones. I feel stones grating dry against my skin, against my teeth.

The older man says, 'Would you have done it, boy? If it had been you there?'

The boy hesitates. 'No.'

'You're lying, boy. Anyone would have done it,' the older man says. 'Anyone. You know. The men marry their selkie brides, and their nets are full and plentiful, and the people of the White Isles eat the fish that they catch. And don't tell me no one knows how cruel it is.' He makes a crude gesture, obscene, with his fingers. 'A woman in your bed at night, her stone face, her stone hands trying to push you away. But she's your luck charm, isn't she?'

The older man says, 'And here's another of my coins to buy another bottle, boy. So we can both drink the thought away.'

They sit side-by-side in the far corner, where the light from the lamp can hardly reach. Piss-stained and bitter and weary. Drink and drink and drink.

'I walk by the sea sometimes,' the older man says. He clutches a stone in his hand tight. 'Looking for her. But only in the day. Maybe I'd ask her to forgive me. Tell her I was ashamed. Help her to find her skin and set her free. But you know, boy, and I know, that's not what I'd do.'

The older man runs his fingers over the stone he's holding. Caresses it. The boy says nothing, and nods his head, and raises the bottle, and drinks.

Knowing Your Type

Eliza Chan

Going to the fair was always a winning date. Knock a few cans over, win an oversized lumpy teddy and suddenly he was a hero. And so inspired, original for not taking them to a restaurant or a bar. Women were always easy to impress.

"Richard-san, look!" Manami said, tugging at his sleeve. She pointed at the brightly lit carousel ride. The horses glistened like glazed doughnuts with swirls of pink and white icing through their manes and tails. They bobbed up and down, impaled on the innocuous gold braids, ever-galloping but never going anywhere.

Manami looked up at him through her thick fringe and a knitted woolen hat. The teddy he had won for her was grotesque. The filling of polystyrene balls pressed against its distended belly and its plastic eyes pointed in different directions. As Manami squeezed it to her side, the seams puckered and strained.

They joined the queue of teenagers and children. Glances were thrown at him, eyes widening when they looked down at his petite date with her pastel blue tights and satchel covered in an oversized lace bow. She was drowning in the sheer volume of clothing—the Asian fashion that swamped her frame. A pretty little china doll.

Manami rummaged in her bag. She pulled out a bejeweled mirror and quickly checked her hair was in place before smiling at him.

"You have the most beautiful eyes," Richard said. Manami looked at him, blushing. "But why don't you wear makeup?"

She nodded apologetically. "I—I have some at home. I'll wear it next time." He watched as she ducked her head.

"And do you own any heels?" he added.

Manami's mouth was hidden in her knitted scarf, but he saw in the satisfaction that her lip quivered. She shuffled in her fabric pumps as if she could hide her feet from sight. Blinking rapidly, the creases in her face smoothed over like remade dough and she pushed a smile into the cracks. She pulled a small cardboard box from her bag. Richard saw his name on top, surrounded by carefully drawn hearts and smiley faces. "I made you some cookies," she said, the diminutive gift shielding her from a further appraisal.

He inspected it, every corner and edge scrutinised by an expert eye. Richard had seen better packaging, origami hearts or a furoshiki-wrapped parcel for example. And there wasn't even a card. He nodded at his date, a non-committal motion of his head.

Inside were a dozen cookies. Lifting one out, he assessed it in the dim light of the carousel bulbs. Generous chocolate chunks began to melt between finger and thumb. He could devour it whole, break from his constructed nonchalance and greedily eat the entire box right now. But that wouldn't do, wouldn't suit the image he had established. The scent of freshly baked warmth lingered like unspoken words between them. Richard snapped the cookie in half. "Share one with me," he said, taking only a tiny bite from the corner.

The cookie was good. It tasted of fervour and anticipation. A little too sweet for his liking but she could be taught, she definitely could be worked on. "It's not bad. Can you cook anything else?"

"Yes, I enjoy cooking! I cook Asian dishes very well, but now I'm learning to cook Western foods too. What is your favourite food? I can learn to make it for you," she said.

"I like lasagne, shepherd's pie, a good Sunday roast, of course. I'll eat Japanese food if you insist, but only once in a while."

Manami's eyes widened and she held her hands up to her mouth as she smiled. "You like Japanese foods? I can make oyakudon and miso soup for you!"

"I'm more open-minded than most," Richard said, "but no seafood." He didn't think it would be appropriate to say that his last three exes had all been Asian. That he had cherry-picked Oriental girls from the dating app.

When the gate opened for them to tumble onto the ride and select their horses, Richard grabbed Manami by the wrist. She looked surprised but did not protest as he pulled her past the nearest horses to a white mare with one cocked hoof and golden hair. Richard let go of her and allowed her to sit side-saddle on the back of the plastic horse. She looked at him strangely then, as if she could not decide whether she liked his audacity or not. But Richard was confident. He had seen it in a Korean drama.

After the ride, they sat in a coffee shop. Manami held a mug of hot chocolate that swamped her lower face. Pink and white marshmallows drowned beneath the mountain of cream. Richard leaned back on the sofa with his tea and admired the view.

"And how has work been?" Manami asked between sips. "Last time you said you were working more from home?"

"Mmm, it's a much more efficient use of my time. Facetime, email - most things can be done with a laptop."

"It sounds very interesting to me. But maybe, a little lonely?"

"How come?"

"Working from home is good for the business. But people need companionship, friends. Otherwise... I mean, would anyone even realise if you were sick?"

Richard laughed. "You're right. It is lonely sometimes. I'm not close to my family anymore." His brow furrowed. "You don't get to my age and position without making some sacrifices, Mana-chan."

The Japanese girl removed her hat and pulled her long black hair over one shoulder. She played with it now, not meeting his eye. "Have you ever been married, Richard-san?"

"Once," he replied, surprising himself with the honest response, "when I was in my twenties."

"She was... English?" Manami asked.

"Scottish. We both prioritised our careers and, well... we drifted apart."

"No children?"

"No." Richard had bumped into his ex-wife only once in recent years. She'd been pushing a pram along the pavement with a gaggle of other mums, clucking away in a language only they seemed to understand. Her hair was scraped back and shadows had taken up residence under her eyes, but she smiled and laughed as she had never done with him. Not even once did she lift her eyes and catch him observing. This was what he had wanted: the housewife, the mother of his children. But she had said no: she was a modern woman with a career. And yet, in the end, as he always knew she would, she had chosen that life. Just with someone else.

"I'm sorry. I've made you sad. Sorry." Manami touched his hand gingerly.

He shook his head, uncertain where the nostalgia had come from. He gave her hand a reassuring squeeze, holding on longer and tighter than was strictly needed. Manami finally broke it off, rubbing her cramped fingers under the table. Richard opened up the checklist he had in his mind, weighing up her strengths and weaknesses with a smack of his lips. It was a most satisfactory outcome.

Richard arrived promptly, ten minutes before they were supposed to meet. He had a dozen red roses and a present wrapped in tissue paper. Tedious and unoriginal and yet that was what they all wanted really. If they were willing to admit it to themselves. Tonight would determine if she met all the requirements, a test Manami was sitting whether she was aware of it or not. She had offered to cook for him and as ever, he would be comparing her skills to his mental checklist. Looking for the jigsaw piece that would fit, even if that meant taking a hacksaw to the edges.

The door was ajar when he arrived. A small furry shape

wedged in the gap. Richard pulled it out. It was a toy rabbit with worn and patchy fur. One of its ears had been mended with awkward stitches. Blue glass eyes bore into him. Richard hefted it under his arm and knocked.

Manami answered the door in a sunflower yellow kitchen apron. The smell of rice wafted into the corridor.

"An escapee?" Richard asked, holding out the plushie.

"Oh, silly me!" Manami said with a light laugh, taking the rabbit from him. She bowed a little, then invited him in. Crossing the threshold, Richard felt a most peculiar sensation. Something pressed again his chest. Shoved him, hard. A gale buffering him back towards the door. He took a step back, stopping only because Manami had grabbed his hand in concern.

"Are you okay?" she asked.

"I— I just feel a little light-headed," he said. He pushed against the resistance, forced stiff legs forward. Heaved and yanked feet of lead. His vision swam whilst a growing whine pierced his ears. Hands pulled him, Manami's voice soothing, through the hallway, guiding him to the living room and sitting him down. The cold glass she pressed against his lips was solid. Hard. The coolness slipped down his throat and his senses gradually re-aligned.

"I'm fine, honestly, just a— a dizzy spell," he said, ignoring rapid punches of adrenaline at his ribcage.

"Are you sure, Richard-san? Do you want to lie down for a moment? Lie down on the couch. It's okay, really, it's okay. I am cooking anyway, so..."

Dimly he felt her take off his shoes and swing his feet up onto her cold leather couch. A moist flannel was pressed on his forehead and then the gentle hands were gone. Richard lay there, staring at the swirls in the artex ceiling and felt like an idiot. He hadn't had a fainting spell since childhood. Perhaps his hours at work were getting too long. He needed someone to take care of him, to cook his dinner and keep his house clean.

Carefully he turned his head to look around. The living room was immaculate. Two cream floor cushions, a low beechwood table, and a sideboard. There were no pictures on the walls, no photos nor ornaments, unusual compared to the other women's houses he had been to.

Only a single glass vase with a cut cherry blossom branch. Some of the blossoms had already wilted and fallen onto the table.

The ringing in his ears had not subsided. Keen whistling. It was like a cold wind punching through his eardrums so that his temples throbbed. He sat up and pressed at the sides of his head.

"How are you feeling?" Manami said, holding a tray of drinks as her slippers slapped across the laminate flooring. She knelt beside him and slid the tray onto the coffee table.

"I'm fine!" Richard lied. Things were not going to plan. He was supposed to take charge of the situation, not the other way around. "Stop fussing."

Manami plucked the errant rabbit plushie where she had dropped it earlier. "Sorry for the mess, I can't keep track sometimes!"

"You have many?" Richard said.

"A few. I guess you could call me a collector. When I'm lonely, I like to cuddle them," Manami said, laughing at herself, "and when I get stressed, or angry, I like to—" She jabbed the rabbit in the face with a little punch, her nose screwed up and her mouth a pout of concentration. Richard laughed along with her. Manami couldn't hurt someone if she tried. "But they keep forever."

"You keep them forever," Richard corrected insistently. Manami had been in the country for a year, and she had said some odd things on their previous dates. It had been endearing at first, but lately, it had started to irritate him. If she wanted to live here, she should learn the language. And the toy collection...? It wasn't a deal-breaker by any means, but it really depended on what she meant by "a few"

"I brought you a present," Richard said.

"Shall I open it?" Manami asked. Her hands already cupped the small parcel he had brought for her. Her fingers were carefully pinched around the curling ends of the decorative ribbon as though they were pinning back the wings of a butterfly.

This is why he liked them, the Asian girls he had dated. Always so submissive, so obedient. "Of course, it's for you," he said.

The heart-shaped pendant hung on a silver chain with a single diamante in it. Manami gasped, her hands covering her mouth. "Oh, Richard, Richard it's... beautiful."

He smiled, helping her clasp it around her neck. Women were magpies, and anything shiny was an easy winner. He had a loyalty card with the jewelry shop; made the most of it with his repeat purchases.

Manami threw her arms around Richard's neck.

"Suki desu," Richard said. The ubiquitous Japanese declaration of love.

Manami pulled away and stared at him in disbelief. "Are you sure?"

"Yes."

The headache pounded at the edges of his vision, but

Richard wasn't going to let it ruin his chances with this girl. His mental checklist was awash with ticks. Sure, he was still dating a Korean girl and messaging a few others, but Manami was close to perfect. Or she would be after he had sandpapered the edges.

Richard did his best to ignore his aching forehead and the sounds that crawled up his neck like fingernails.

Manami bent in to kiss him.

He must have blanked out.

Chopsticks lay in his hands and half a bowl of rice in front of him. Manami smiled at him across the kitchen table. A bitter taste filled his mouth and the crumbs of a finished dish lay scattered on a patterned blue plate before him. The kitchen behind Manami was cluttered with opened jars and unwashed plates. She was a messy cook, although there was not a single pan on the cooker. Manami scooped more of the dish up from a large bowl. She dumped a mass of congealed beige before him. Looked expectant, adoring.

Pretending confidence, Richard picked up a sizeable portion and shovelled it into his mouth. It tasted of nothing. Like candy floss dissolving on his palate but without the sweetness. Strands clung to the roof of his mouth, and he drained his glass to push it down.

"That should be enough," Manami said.

"What, erm, was that dish?"

"Silly, I've told you already!" she said, twirling the pendant he had given her.

"Such an, um, unusual name though," Richard said.

"In English, it is translated as 'filled up'? You know, your stomach. Oh, I mean stuffing, that's it, stuffing! For the chicken, the Christmas one."

"Do you mean like sausage meat for the turkey?"

Manami shook her head, "No, not meat. It's not a British dish... it's a family recipe." Her lower lip quivered. "You said you liked it, don't you?"

"Of yes, it was fine, but next time I come you should make steak and chips," Richard said.

"Next time," Manami echoed, smiling with her teeth. The way she said it was less in agreement but something else. A slight curve of mockery? No, he must be imagining it. She struggled to understand humour at the best of times.

But she did not hunch over and look at her lap anymore. Straight-backed, Manami held his eye until he was the one to turn away. Her clothes had changed too. The pretty dress and apron had been replaced by a stained T-shirt and leggings. It was not a look he went for.

Something distracted him from his musings. An itch on his leg. He rubbed his ankles together. It subsided for a moment and then he felt it again. Glancing under the table, Richard found the toy rabbit again. Richard stared at it in confusion.

Manami grabbed it up and stroked the rabbit's head. "Silly. We'll have to fix you up."

"I, uh, just need to use your bathroom," Richard said, standing up from the table. He closed the kitchen door firmly behind him. Looking around, Richard headed straight for Manami's bedroom. He needed to check what the damage was. A few toys he could handle, but ...

Her bedroom was cream and pink with heart-shaped cushions piled up on the bed. In contrast to the living room, it was a very messy space. Richard warily stepped between the discarded clothes and pieces of fluff that littered the floor. On the dressing table, a sewing box lay splayed open. He ran his fingers through the clutter of needles and thread, plastic spools rolling haphazardly although he could not see a sewing machine nor any craft projects. Nor any toys for that matter.

Richard glanced back at the kitchen door before crossing the room to the built-in wardrobe. At first, the louvered cream doors were stiff when he pulled them. He yanked hard, falling back against the corner of the bed as they finally creaked open. Three shelves of plushies filled the wardrobe: cats, dogs, teddies, a veritable menagerie of soft lifeless faces. A yellow duck with a crooked beak, a discoloured cat with a crudely restitched tail, three chipmunks with grimaces sewn ear to ear. There was a blob shaped like a sad teardrop and a star with an inane grin. A penguin with its mouth agape rolled across the carpet and stared up at him.

He heard feet moving behind the kitchen door and the handle began to turn. Richard raced across the bedroom and into the bathroom, locking the door behind him. Gripping the sink, he looked at himself in the mirror. His vision blurred over and refocused. The room swayed like after a heavy night of drinking. His eyes were bloodshot and his reflection lurched towards him. So, she liked to practise stitching on her toys. He thought about the other reasons he had stopped dating girls and tried to put this along the hierarchy. Tried, and failed.

"Come on Richard, pull yourself together," he whispered to the glass. Straightening up, he cleared his throat and tried to look convincing. Picked a piece of fluff from his collar, another from his hair. His hand hovered over the bin. It was full: filled entirely with fluff: soft and cotton-like, all of it stained like rust with dried blood.

He crouched, heart, thudding so loud that he could

hear it ringing in his ears. He swallowed, but his throat was scratched dry with the remnants of the meal. He turned on the tap and splashed water on his face, scooped handfuls of it into his mouth greedily and hoping the cold water would calm his nerves. There had to be a rational explanation. Women had... periods. Disgusting though, for her to leave it out like that. But that was all it was.

A steady dripping sound entered his consciousness. He had turned off the water but there it was. Tap, tap, tapping. Richard looked at himself in the mirror, the water clinging to his short hair like sweat beads. Noticed for the first time the drawn shower curtain behind him. His eyes looked back, daring him.

It was like the white curtain around hospital cubicles. The rings scraped against the rail, a harsh metallic clank like manacles snapping shut. Three toy carcasses lay across a drying rack, limp and skinned. They had been turned inside out and every shred of stuffing removed. The dripping came from the leg of the last toy. The bear he had won at the fair. Its paunch sagged with excess skin and those inverted beady eyes stared at him. The liquid pooled onto the white enamel, a red stream idly dribbling down the drain.

Richard backed up until he stood against the wall. He stared at the skins, clutching for a logical explanation. His head ran through his mental checklists, switched it to a barchart, a sliding scale. It fell right off the end and kept running. His head pulsed with one repeated scream. Get out.

Carefully opening the bathroom door, Richard looked into the hallway. The kitchen was round the corner and Manami would never know. He inched his way into the hall. He just needed to grab his shoes.

Each time he looked down, dark spots filled his vision and he had to stop. Richard squeezed his eyes shut and told himself to just get out. Barefooted if necessary. He opened his eyes again and took the last few steps, his hands reaching for the deadlock. Something blocked his way.

Shoes. Leather brogues in tan and black, dirty trainers, suede loafers and espadrilles were heaped up all around the door. All men's shoes, his included, removed on entry and never reclaimed. The errant rabbit plushie sat atop the heap, watching him.

"You can't leave," Manami said from behind him. "We haven't had dessert."

Richard waded through the shoes and yanked at the lock: twisting it, shaking it to no avail.

"You said you'd teach me to be a good girlfriend. Fix me." Her voice was directly behind him now, right by his ear.

"You have toy skins…"

Her hands were on his shoulders and she spun him around slowly. Manami was holding the bear. It was nothing more than a skinned pelt, folded over on itself, limbs waving uselessly to and fro. Richard's own full stomach protested.

"I like to repair things too, you see. The defective ones, the ones that tick my list," Manami said. She stood with a hand on her hip looking down at him. Richard's stomach cramped and he bent over, bowing to her despite himself. She was nothing more than a petite Asian girl. He could handle her.

The cramp passed and Richard pulled himself back up. "I don't know what sort of perversion you are into but that's enough. Unlock this door right now and—" He stopped, mouth dry, and gagged. Something caught in his throat. Richard tried to swallow the bile back down but the feeling was overwhelming. He vomited. The contents of his stomach spilt over the strangers' shoes, over the welcome mat and his own feet. Gasping as he finished, he stared down at the mess. It was stuffing. White downy stuffing. His whole chest had caved in.

"Now I fix you," Manami said. She crouched down beside him, a threaded needle in her hand. Richard looked up, surprised as she loomed above him.

He tried to shove her away. Stubby limbs flapped ineffectively. Too short to push, too weak to offer any resistance. They merely waved at her arm, tickling her. He stared at the stumps, open-mouthed, trying, again and again, to curl and uncurl his fingers. His ears rang with a voiceless scream.

"What...I...no... Now listen to me, girl!" he started.

Manami clamped her hand over his mouth. Her hand was so big it covered his whole face, squashing the soft fur around his cheeks. Richard scrambled in panic, shaking his head although his eyes were rivetted in place: glued to her face, to the contemplative tilt of her head as she examined the problem from each angle. He scrunched his eyes closed. It was just a dream. A nightmare.

Blinked again.

And again.

But on the third time, his eyes would not close. They were locked open, pupils dilated into perfectly round plastic beads.

"First thing's first." She started to sew his mouth shut.

Little Bear

Avra Margariti

Bear? I ask my traveling companion. My teeth chatter so hard I'm afraid they'll chop off my tongue.

"Yes, Girl?"

"Will we be there soon?"

"You will know when we reach the end."

All of Bear's words sound wise. She speaks in a growl that starts deep in her chest and rolls all the way up her throat. I can feel its rumbling echo; the baby inside me feels it too and stirs. I tap a soothing rhythm against my rounded belly—ba-dum, ba-dum,—like a heartbeat.

The whole world stings white and hazy. Sometimes I try to catch a glimpse of the sky through the mist that veils my eyes, but mostly, I focus on setting my own feet in Bear's deep paw prints in the luminous snow. It's easy to get lost forever in this weather, so easy to stumble and never get back up.

Bear turns around and noses my side, a warm, familiar pressure. I plod on through the barren landscape. What for, I don't know. But then the baby gives a sudden kick, as if to remind me.

Most woodland creatures are deep in hibernation. Those still awake avoid me, but they seem especially reluctant to find themselves in Bear's path. It's like they can somehow sense her otherness. I see the small birds and rodents out of the corner of my eye; they flitter between the skeletal tree branches and scamper in the scarce, needlepoint vegetation when we walk past their nests and burrows.

The burn in my feet starts dull, but soon every step is a razor cut. We take shelter from the icy wind behind some boulders jutting out of the earth like crooked teeth.

While Bear hunts, I start a fire using twigs, a sputtering lighter, and pages ripped from an old *Hunter's Handbook*. I unlace my boots and peel off my wet socks. My ankles are purple-veined, swollen. My blisters ooze blood. I shuffle around to get comfortable in the giant coat I'd stolen from the cabin in the mountains. I had to roll it around in the snow to rid it of the tobacco stink that made my stomach wrench worse than morning sickness.

The fire spits and crackles feebly. The crystallized snowflakes on my lashes melt tears into my eyes.

When Bear returns, I ask, "Am I—are we lost?"

She says, "What has been lost can never be returned."

"That's not what I asked."

Bear smiles. Her lips stretch to expose blackened gums and gleaming yellow teeth. I don't recoil at the stench of animal musk and decay.

LITTLE BEAR

I retrieve a can of baked beans from my rucksack and stare at the grub-like pellets. I haven't had a hot meal since I ran away from the cabin almost a month ago.

Bear nudges her snout against my frozen backside. "Eat. You need to keep your strength up. Do it for your cub."

My cub. My baby. My little bear.

I spoon some of the pasty beans into my mouth. My baby's kicks bounce against my inner walls. "You like that?" I coo around a bite. "You like beans?"

Bear stops tearing into the moose carcass she dragged to our campsite and watches me with her dark, dark eyes. There are guts caught between her teeth. Pink and wet, they glisten in the firelight as though they hold omens inside their folds.

"Have you picked a name for her?" Bear asks.

"How do you know it's a girl?"

"A mother knows these things." Bear's grunt sounds baleful, but I recognize it for what it is.

Sadness.

I don't know who the father is. If it's my own old dad or one of the gin-drinking, tobacco-chewing hunters from back in the cabin. I had been a runaway for less than a week before the three hunters picked me up in their truck. They pulled up beside me while I was searching for roadkill along the salt-brined highway. "Looks like we've caught ourselves a rabbit," they chuckled, and I did feel like a rabbit then, like something small and animalistic under the weight of their leers and gropes.

Bear stretches on her back, ferns and dull-brown pine needles flattened beneath her massive body. I huddle closer to her. The forest animals might not recognize Bear as their own, but I've felt a kinship with her. It's under my breastbone, in my heart, this knowledge that wilts away when I try to put it into words.

The blustering wind picks up and blows thick whorls of snow our way. A wet cough rattles my lungs. I muffle my wheezing against Bear's warm side and comb numb fingers through her bristled fur, working the kinks out of the long, wild tufts. She lets me, although sometimes I think it hurts her. It's not a physical ache. This pain hits somewhere else, somewhere deeper. Somewhere inside.

After the storm passes that night, the sky is the clearest it's been in days. The horizon is so enormous, it could swallow us whole. Not for the first time, I notice the Bears above are missing. The men in the cabin told stories about them. Ursa Major and Ursa Minor: the Great and the Small Bear. You could once find them by spotting the Big Dipper or Polaris, the North Star.

When I first asked Bear about the empty patch of the night sky, she snarled and refused to talk about it. But now, dozing in my sleeping bag beneath the stars, I hear her lift her heavy head from her front paws and say, "The little bear, she went missing first, so it was up to the big bear to climb down from the sky and look for her cub on earth."

I hum a little song for the baby sleeping inside me. "Yet all you found was me."

Bear looks at my belly full as the moon. "One day, Girl. One day you'll understand the sacrifices we're all called to make."

I realize the tune I'm murmuring came from the men in the cabin. My voice falters and splits, the words frost-sharp on my tongue. I already understand, but I don't tell Bear that.

"You've been watching over me for weeks. What about your own cub? Your search?"

Don't you miss the sky? I want to ask, but the wind snatches my words away.

Bear cranes her neck toward the yawning darkness, devoid of two of its many star clusters. Her smile is like the barrel of a gun.

"Wherever my cub is now, she's long gone." Then, quietly: "I can never return to the sky. There must always be two bears."

And that's when my water breaks.

It iss slow at first, and then it's fast and wet and violent. Bear lets me lean against her as I pant and shiver. It's as if I'm being torn apart from the inside, and I don't know if my body can take it.I Don't know if I can put myself back together afterwards.

The first thing my screaming, thrashing daughter sees of this world is snow. I cut the umbilical cord with my teeth. Bear's coarse tongue licks my sweat-slick face; her hot breath fans over the red-faced, bloodied baby bundled up in fleece and fur. For an inexplicable moment, the instinct to scratch and claw—to protect my baby from Bear—overtakes me, but that too passes as the world swims in and out of focus and everything is white, so white.

And red.

"You did it," Bear says.

For the first time in all these months, I let myself admit it: "I wasn't sure I could."

I hadn't planned to give birth in this blizzard-ravaged wasteland. I thought I'd stay in the cabin until I had my baby, then run away afterward. But then I couldn't lie still and silent anymore like all those dead-eyed animals mounted on the cabin walls. I couldn't look at the loaded rifles and not imagine the hunters sending a bullet through my baby's soft skull.

I unzip my coat and expose my tender breasts for my daughter to latch onto. The wind's kiss has frigid teeth, but it's okay. My body is too tired to shiver.

Sometime during the night, my daughter stops crying. Then she stops moving. I only allow myself a few tears. Even those turn to ice halfway down my cheeks. All the while, Bear watches me silently, a mournful look in her eyes.

* * *

We travel on. Time turns in on itself, folds and unfurls like springtime flowers; like the far-off memory of them.

Finally, I drop to my knees and croak, "I can't keep going." The whiteness eats up my voice, but Bear hears me anyway.

"We're here," she says.

Here is a snow-capped cliff. Roiling fog and jagged emptiness below, clear sky sprawling endlessly above. The patch of missing stars is right in front of me. If I reach out, I might dip my fingers into the black of the sky.

My baby is a cold thing, a dead weight, but I don't let go of her. When I'm at the cliff's edge, I turn around to Bear for guidance, but she's no longer with me. Only her voice remains, that deep, comforting growl, followed by another softer, younger yap. "You know what to do, Girl."

The two voices fade before disappearing altogether. Despite everything, I'm happy for Bear. Somewhere beyond earth or sky, she's reunited with her cub at last.

I look back at the sky; at the embroidery of stars

shining bright against the inky canvas. At the void where the constellations, Ursa Major and Ursa Minor, should be. *There must always be two bears.*

I hug my baby—my cub—to my chest and step forward. Together, we float up into the sky.

Till the Very End of Days

by T.A. Sola

My father disappeared late in the winter, when the days were still short and gray and bone-achingly cold.

We argued on our last night together. I thought myself old enough to join him on a hunt to find and kill the wolf prowling around the village and preying on newborn lambs, but it seemed my father had little faith in the skills he'd taught his son.

"The wolf is desperate," he told me while sharpening his boar-spear by the oven's light. "It is alone and starving, and that makes it dangerous. Too dangerous for me to take you along, Vasile."

"But you think you can kill it on your own?" I'd been soaking his boots with birch oil, but now I tossed them to the ground and threw the tin into the oven. It popped and sputtered and filled the cottage with black, stinking smoke.

He didn't look up from his spear. My father rarely lost his temper, and it seemed this night was no exception. "Yes. I have some experience with this, boy."

"You're a miller." I spat out the words like an insult, and I meant them as such. What could a man who spent his days slaving at a millstone possibly know about tracking and killing a wolf? He had taught me to hunt, yes, but only squirrels and rabbits and boars.

"I wasn't always," he said. I didn't know what he meant, but I was too angry to ask. All I could do was cross my arms and scowl, and hope my poor job oiling his boots would leave his feet cold and wet.

A childish thought, I know, and I realized later it wasn't truly anger I felt toward my father. I was worried for him, afraid he'd go off into the forest and never return. I didn't want him to face the wolf alone, and I thought that bringing even me, a boy of sixteen summers, would be better than bringing no one at all.

I should have told him as much when he climbed from his bed the next morning. But I didn't. I was too ashamed of the things I'd said the night before, so I stayed still and silent when he pushed open the door and stepped out into the frigid morning air.

He stopped and looked back into the cottage. Perhaps he thought me still asleep, or saw my eyes were open but mistook the worry in them for anger. Either way, he turned and shut the door without a word, and that brief, fuzzy glimpse of his face was the last I ever saw of him.

I found his hunting knife later that spring, its blood-crusted blade driven into the trunk of a felled tree. I thought it a sign that my father was truly dead, that I should let go of the little scrap of hope I had been clinging to. That I should pick up the pieces of my life and try to move on.

But there were others who thought differently. They whispered about the knife, the blood, the strangeness of the whole affair. Perhaps, had I listened more closely to their tales, I would not find myself where I am today. Trapped in the cold and the dark. Locked away till the very end of days.

* * *

The years that followed were difficult ones, but I did my best to run the mill as my father had taught me. And while the flour I ground might not have been as fine as his, and the bread I baked not so soft and crusty, I did a decent enough job that no one complained too loudly.

Not until the grain ran out, at least.

The land had always been good to us, the soil made rich and fertile by the river. But a dry autumn delayed the planting of our fall grains, and an early winter with too little snow killed off the seedlings that hadn't had time to root.

Our situation did not improve come spring. Heavy rains swelled the river and flooded the plains whose grass we used for fodder, and our animals, damned to suffer the same hunger-filled days as their masters, were slaughtered for their meat when they grew too sickly to plough the fields.

We might have saved ourselves had we been able to

trade the coal our miners pulled from the rugged hills at the base of the mountains. But the rains had made the river a wild, dangerous thing, and the keelboats we sent out never returned. More than a few were found capsized or beached on the river's muddy banks with no sign of the men or women who had manned them.

"It's not the river doing these evil deeds," Dimitri said one night as we tried to drink away the pain from our empty stomachs. He was a fisherman with too few fish to catch now that everyone with a net had taken to the streams and lakes to keep their families fed. "I've heard the singing late at night, Vasile. Seen the shadows on the riverbank. It's the rusalki and their ilk causing us these woes."

"They've never troubled us before," I told him, though I didn't give much credence to his superstitious talk. My thoughts were crowded with more pressing concerns. I had little time for tales of water nymphs and demons.

The rains ended early that summer. What followed were five of the hottest, driest months I had ever known, and with them died any hope of salvaging our crops. People started to whisper of famine, and their fear and hunger drove them to my doorstep where they demanded I give them bags of wheat, barley, and rye.

"I've nothing left to give you," I told the angry crowd. These were folk I had known all my life, but I didn't recognize them now. Their faces were scowls, their voices full of hate. Hunger had turned them into something else.

A short, scrawny farmer stepped to the front of the group and pointed his scythe at my chest. "Every time we bring our grain for grinding, you set aside a little something for yourself. Bring it out to us, boy, or we'll be going in and taking it for ourselves."

It's true I took a portion of their crop as payment for its milling, but I'd already shared out what little had remained of those stores. "It's gone," I said. "Made into the breads and porridges I brought into the village not two weeks ago." I pointed at Tierney, the potter's wife, who had always been kind to me. "Is your mind so addled by hunger that you've forgotten the bread I brought to your children?"

She refused to answer my question or to look me in the eye. I realized, then, that nothing I could say would get through to them. They thought me a thief and a liar, and the only way to prove the truth of my words was to let them inside to see for themselves.

Dimitri found me later that evening as I struggled to fix the millstone unseated during the looting. He looked around, his eyes hard as he surveyed the damage, before resting his hand on my back. "I'll be sleeping here for a while," he told me. "Best you aren't alone if the bastards come back to set the place afire."

He stayed with me through the inevitable famine that spread across the land that year. For a time, we had fresh fish and wild game to put on our table, but meat became scarce as more folk turned to the wilderness for sustenance. We were forced to eat bark bread, then, a vile concoction of weeds and chopped straw, cockle and tree bark, and sometimes, if things were particularly dire, sand.

It filled our bellies. Kept us alive. But it did nothing to help fight the despair that gnawed at our minds nearly every waking hour. It became a struggle to even crawl out of bed in the morning, yet we forced ourselves to do exactly that.

We were survivors, Dimitri and I, but there were others who were not. Those that couldn't find the will to keep going, who knew that they were starving and faced an agonizing death, chose instead to give themselves to the river. An easier, gentler fate than the one they would have otherwise faced.

They couldn't have known their deaths would nearly damn us all.

* * *

On a cold night in autumn, an inhuman screech shook me from a restless sleep. For a moment I thought I had imagined it, that it was just another nightmare conjured up by my food-starved mind, but the screech rang out again, much closer this time, and it made the fine hairs on the back of my neck stand on end.

Dimitri lay beside me on a cot too small for both our frames. I could feel every one of his ribs where his body pressed against mine, could see in the gauntness of his cheeks beneath his scruffy, unkempt beard, and the sharp edge of his collarbone bit into my palm when I squeezed his shoulder to wake him.

"What is it?" he mumbled, his voice heavy with sleep. "Another dream?"

"No. There's something outside. Down near the river, I think." I told him to stay still and listen, but the only sounds to be heard were the chirping of crickets and the rustling of leaves. Dimitri looked up at me, and I could tell by the worry in his eyes that he thought my sickness had started to affect my mind.

I'd lost two teeth earlier that week. My gums were sore and bleeding, my skin pale and blotchy. I could not rid my bones of their constant, throbbing ache, and I'd been plagued by a fever that left me shivering and sweating. But I was not hallucinating. My thoughts, though slow and sluggish, were still my own.

"Just wait," I said, and not a heartbeat passed before that horrible shriek echoed through the trees again.

Dimitri's quiet curse sent a trickle of unease down my spine. "What is it?" I asked him. "What's making that noise?"

"A rusalka." He went over to the window to close and bolt the shutters, then rummaged for his trousers in the dark. "More than one from the sound of it. They're bold to stray this close to the village, or perhaps they are just opportunistic."

I shook my head and wanted to tell him it was only an animal, but no fox or bear could possibly make such a noise. There was an otherness to those shrieks, a wrongness that made my eyes itch and my heart pound painfully in my chest. In the end, I could only ask, "What do we do?"

"Drive them away," he said. "And quickly. More will come if they are not silenced."

"More? How many can there be?"

"As many as there were folk who drowned themselves in the river." He sat beside me to pull on his boots, and I did not like the grim look I saw upon his face. "Rusalki aren't the pretty maidens from the folktales, Vasile. Men, women, children... It matters not what they were before they walked into the river. They'll be twisted and changed and having a taste for flesh, and the sooner we can be rid of them the better off we'll be."

I had no experience with such things, so I let Dimitri pour candle wax into my ears—protection from the rusalka's song, he claimed—and arm me with a boar-spear, and together we made our way down to the river's edge to confront a creature I had thought existed only in fishermen's tales.

But an exhaustive search of the riverbank uncovered nothing more threatening than a heron picking its way through the reeds. I started to feel foolish for having dragged Dimitri from his bed, and I could not help but wonder if I'd allowed my feverish imaginings to get the better of us both.

"We should go home," I finally said. "I'll come back in the morning to search for tracks." I did not expect to find any, but perhaps I would discover a more rational explanation behind the noises we had heard.

Dimitri did not look ready to give up the search, but he surprised me by nodding and wrapping his arm around my waist. "You are right, solnyhko. There's not much we can do if they do not wish to be seen."

I leaned against him, more heavily than I had intended, but my knees were weak, and I could not catch my breath. The scurvy was killing me. Slowly, yes, but I'd be dead within a month—and Dimitri not far behind me—if we could not find fresh fruits or meat.

These thoughts weighed heavily on my mind as we walked back up the muddy, tree-lined path, and they pushed aside any lingering concerns I might have had about the rusalki or strange noises in the night. So it came as a surprise when, after a trickle of water dripped onto the back of my neck, I glanced up into the trees to see a still and silent monster crouched on a branch just above our heads.

The beast moved with a frightening speed. By the time I managed to shout a panicked warning it had already leapt from the branch, wrapped its spindly arms around Dimitri's waist, and sunk its teeth deep into his side. I watched, eyes wide and jaw slack, as the thing tore free a ragged chunk of his flesh and swallowed it whole.

Dimitri's screams, dulled by the wax plugging my ears, shook me from my stupor, and I thrust my spear's sharpened tip into the demon's back. It shrieked and hissed and slashed at me with its cracked and broken nails, but I knocked it to the ground and stabbed it in the chest, over and over and over again until its ear-splitting screams died in its throat and it lay twitching and jerking in the mud.

I saw the rusalka's face, then. A familiar face despite the milky white eyes and rotted nose, and seeing it, recognizing it, caused something inside me to break. I slammed the spear's haft into its ugly, misshapen skull, struck it again and again until I could no longer see even a hint of the child it had been.

I do not remember dragging Dimitri back to the cottage or stretching him out on the table beside the warmth of the oven. I can only recall his face, pale as freshly fallen snow, and the blood that seeped from the ragged hole in his side. So much blood that I thought for certain he would die.

But he didn't. I wonder now if he wished he had.

* * *

The summer before he disappeared, I woke early one morning to find my father standing at the edge of the millpond with a dozen or more buttons clutched in his hands. He had cut them from our coats and trousers, and I watched, confused and more than a little worried, as he tossed them into the water while muttering words in a language I did not understand.

"What are you doing?" I asked him.

"We had a visitor last night." He nodded toward a section of the dam where the stones had cracked and splintered. "Did you not hear it trying to tear apart our dam?"

A crash had startled me awake not long after I'd drifted to sleep, but there had been a storm earlier in the day, and the trees round the mill were old and prone to falling. I pointed to the trunk bobbing below the water's surface and said, "It was just a tree. The wind must have loosened its roots."

"The tree fell, that's true, but it wasn't the wind that brought it down. It was the vodyanoy. The little devil's trying to make its home in our millpond."

He shuffled the buttons in his hand and watched the log bump against the dam's broken stonework. "Don't ever let it stay, boy. If you have the misfortune of seeing one, you find yourself some buttons and throw them into the water to drive the beast away."

The look on my face made him frown. He knelt beside me, put a hand on my shoulder and squeezed. "Listen to me, boy, and closely. The vodyanoy collects souls, for power and for wealth. It'll trick you into thinking it's friendly by keeping the river calm and your water wheel turning, but soon enough you'll find yourself drowning drunks or weary travelers as payment to the bastard. And do you know what will happen if you don't?"

I didn't want to know, didn't believe a single word he'd said, but he waited, silent, until I asked, "What?"

"It'll seal away your soul in a pretty porcelain cup."

I'd thought him mad that day. But now, after having killed a rusalka with my own two hands, I knew he'd been telling me the truth.

The vodyanoy was real, and I thought perhaps it could save us all.

* * *

"I have to do it," I said to Dimitri. The herbs I'd packed into his wound had stopped the thin tendrils of infection from creeping across his belly and up into his chest, but I didn't think it would truly start to heal until he regained some of the strength he'd lost over these long, hard months of famine. He needed hearty meals and restful nights, and it seemed unlikely he'd get either unless I did something, anything to improve our situation.

Killing Tierney's boy—for that's who the rusalka had been, a lad no more than eight summers old—had not kept the rusalki away. They were everywhere now, roaming the riverbanks and flitting through the trees, and it had been too long since their awful songs hadn't plagued our days and nights.

"You don't." He grasped my hand and gave it a gentle squeeze. "Just leave, Vasile. Go south toward the coast and escape this hell."

"No." I took a damp rag from the basin beside the cot and wiped the sweat from his face. "There's game returning to the forest, Dimitri. Fish to the river. If this works, if the life I take brings the vodyanoy to us and convinces him to drive away the rusalki, then we'll have everything we need to survive."

"It's more than just her life you'll be taking." He took the rag from his forehead and tossed it onto the floor. "The folktales have it wrong about the rusalki. What makes you think it'll be any different for the vodyanoy?"

"Maybe it won't, but we're dying all the same. What harm is there in seeing for ourselves?"

"She's an old woman, Vasile."

"Who's lost her family and wants only to die." He hadn't been there when I'd found her in the village, old and alone and choking on a mouthful of moldy straw while she prayed for a swift, clean end. Killing her would be a mercy. "I'll do it now, before the sun rises."

I started for the door, but he caught my sleeve and pulled me close, so close our cheeks were touching. "Be careful, solnishko. Making a deal with a chyert is a dangerous thing."

The warmth of his breath lingered on my skin long after I went to the mill and took the old woman into my arms. I carried her down to the millpond, and she smiled a toothless grin as I waded out into the frigid water.

"It will be alright, majka," I said. "You'll be with your grandchildren soon." A lie, but I did not want her last moments to be clouded by fear.

I lowered her into the water, gently, until her head slipped below the millpond's glassy surface. Then I held her there, my hands wrapped tightly around her scrawny shoulders, until the thrashing stopped, her body stilled, and the vodyanoy came crawling from the river to claim her soul.

*　*　*

A single soul gave the vodyanoy the power to drive the rusalki away. It wouldn't last, he warned me that night he appeared, so I promised him more, a new one each year, in return for his continued protection. He agreed, and though he was a frightening thing to look upon with his frog-like face and eyes that glowed like burning coals, not once did he break his word.

He kept us safe from the rusalki. And though I cannot say if he intended it, his very presence—which grew with every soul he sealed away in his strange collection of mismatched porcelain cups—seemed to breathe new life into the land.

We could hunt again. Fish again. Even the mines were reopened, and in time we sent keelboats laden with coal to those distant cities the famine had never reached. Not only did we survive, but we prospered, and I cannot say I regret the price I had to pay for it. Not with Dimitri healed and strong and back on the river, plying his trade.

It is true he did not smile quite as often as he once had, and that sometimes, late at night while the fire in the oven snapped and popped and crackled, he would become quiet and withdrawn. But I had him by my side, had his love despite all the lives I'd taken, and that was enough for me.

I thought, naively, those days would last forever. But one Midsummer's Eve, while I watched the vodyanoy claim yet another soul, a familiar howl echoed through the forest. I turned to see a wolf sprinting from the trees, and I moved, unthinking, to shield the vodyanoy from the beast's attack.

The wolf's jaws closed around my throat. It released me almost instantly, but its teeth had sunk too deep.

I collapsed into the millpond's shallow water, blood leaking from my torn throat. I tried to picture Dimitri's face, wanted it to be the last image in my mind when death came to claim me, but the wolf would not grant me this final gift. It licked my hands and nudged at my face, and when I turned my head, I found it staring down at me with my father's bright blue eyes.

I knew, then, that he'd only meant to protect me from the chyert, the vodyanoy, as his kind were said to do.

"You came back," I said, and I was glad to have seen him, so changed and yet familiar, one last time before the world went dark.

I will never forget the yelp and whine that followed, or the feeling of the vodyanoy's arms, slick with blood that was not my own, wrapped tightly around me.

* * *

I can't say how many times I've told myself this story. A hundred? A thousand? More, perhaps. But the memories within it are all I have left, and I feel them slipping away with every passing season.

What will happen when they are gone, when I've forgotten Dimitri and my father and the feel of the sun on my skin? Will I still exist in this dark, endless void, or will my soul simply cease to be?

I hope it is the latter, but I do not expect such a mercy. I have damned too many people to this hell. Why should I be the one to escape it?

No, I think it likely I will be here forever. Alone and unremembering, trapped for an eternity in a tiny porcelain cup.

Redundancy of Yellow Flower Tea

by Luke Frostick

A tax collector's life is a lonely one, but Ume-Hana had rarely felt as empty as she did on Grey Thrush Island.

Grey Thrush Island was the furthest point of the southeastern archipelago. Ume-Hana didn't know if this was the most remote part of the kingdom, but it couldn't be far from it. As the gaps between the islands stretched out, trade dwindled. Each island she came to felt lonelier, poorer until the peasants were left scratching out an existence from fishing, a few animals and what rice or millet they could grow.

On Grey Thrush Island, they didn't even bother with smuggling. There was nothing to smuggle. The Iron Boat's captain didn't expect to do much in the way of trade. He made more money transporting the monks drawn to the island in search of yellow flower tea famous for its prothetic properties.

Ume-Hana'd been working her way south for the whole of the summer, catching the smoke-belching Iron Boats that ran trade runs, mostly in dry fish, between the little fishing villages. Every time she reached a village, she scraped what measly taxes she could out of them then moved on. It almost didn't seem worth the bother. Yet she knew that the Daimyo's duty had to be carried out.

Ume-Hana hated the way they stared at her and the fear in their eyes when they spotted her tax collector's insignia. It hadn't bothered her in the past; duty had been enough, but she'd been meandering through the islands for thirty-five years now and was fast running out of spirit.

She wasn't the only thing that had changed. When she was younger, she'd moved on nimble skiffs and catamarans that had danced across the water. Now, she only traveled on Iron Boats that chugged across the water like it was treacle, leaving a black streak across the sky and a foul trail in the sea.

This journey had been unpleasant. The constant noise of the Iron Boat had grated on her. Every wave made the Iron Boat list and bellyflop into the waves with painful slaps of water and metal. It made her feel queasy, something a life on the sea had thus far inoculated her against. The smoke from the coal engine left black residue under her nails and made her cough. To get away from the stench, she looked out to the sea, but that came with its own trials. The ocean, which had always teemed with life, was now empty except for the jellyfish the propeller pulped. Not a single turtle's head bobbed above the water; the flying fish didn't dance in the spray, and no dolphins came to play in the wake. Even the gulls looked greasy and bedraggled. The quality of the sea had weighed heavily on Ume-Hana's mind. Nobody at the Daimyo's castle thought there was a problem, let alone that they should look for a cause.

A three-day journey took them Grey Thrush Island across the lethargic sea without a breeze to cool her. It was pretty much uneventful, except for a strange happening on the second day. As she stared into the sea, a shadow passed beneath her, deep in the water. It was at least the same size as the boat but traveled with a predatory grace that defied its bulk. It slipped past them like ink running across stone and disappeared out of Ume-Hana's vision. An omen, she thought and shivered despite the oppressive heat.

* * *

There were two villages on Grey Thrush Island - The Beak and The Tail. The boat docked in the sharped edged harbour of The Beak, and Ume-Hana was met by the local head-woman, Kurushimi. The headman was away at sea, acting as the captain of the island's singular Iron Boat, leaving the head-woman in charge.

As Ume-Hana hadn't been to this Island before, formal introductions were held in the village hall, a simple wooden building with a thatched roof and rotten tatami mats.

They discussed the day's business over tea. It was bitter and heavily cut with brown rice in an attempt to make the valuable brew last longer.

Kurushimi bustled despite the heat. Quite capable of handling the headman's duty, she presented the Daimyo's taxes dutifully collected in the last three years since Ume-Hana had visited.

The collection was low. Abysmally low. Ume-Hana put the few coins in her strongbox and locked it up tight.

She hadn't expected great riches from that most remote island, but still, so few coins was unprecedented. "Why is there so little?" Ume-Hana asked, knowing the answer all too well.

"Times have been hard. They have been for some time." Kurushimi told her. "The men go out on the Iron Boat, but the catches grow smaller and smaller, and they have to range further and further to feed us."

Ume-Hana had heard the same story from other villages on her journey through the heat and humidity of the archipelago. She voiced her sympathies as she noted the takings down in her ledger. The taxes that the villages were struggling to pay off totalled less than the gold insignia strapped to her arm. She felt nauseous at how deeply the head-woman bowed after Ume-Hana forgave a third of their debts.

"It's not just the men out on the deep sea," Kurushimi continued. "We women feel it too. When we dive, we have to go deep to find the shellfish that used to fill the shallows. We pull them up, but have to cook them through because they go bad in the warm seawaters. The corrals we search round have turned white, and more often than not we come up with nothing more than gashes on our hands and feet. That, Official, brings the sharks. They are hungry and aggressive. It's dangerous work for little reward."

"Everybody knows that the diving women of Grey Thrush Island are amongst the bravest in the land." It was a platitude Ume-Hana told to head-women across the archipelago, but Kurushimi seemed to appreciate it.

"Small catches are bad, Official, but there is more. The sea itself is sick. I honestly believe it. When we dive, Official, we come up stinking of decay. When I was a girl, I remember my mother's skin smelt of pure salt more beautiful than any rich woman's perfume. Now we spend hours in the hot springs trying to get the smell of rot out of our hair."

Again, this wasn't news to Ume-Hana. Over the past year, she had found that many of the bays that she had swum in as a child now repulsed her and jellyfish clogged the mouths of once pristine harbours.

* * *

With her business finished, she started to walk to The Tail. Nobody in The Beak had been willing to take her round in a boat. After all, what kind of person would inflict a tax collector on their neighbour? They told her that their Iron Boat was out in the deep sea chasing the shoals of fish and added that all the sailing ships were needed for the diving women. The captain of the Iron Boat that brought them to the island couldn't be persuaded either. He was keen to be away to more profitable harbours.

"Don't worry," they had told her. "There is a path and you can stop for a night's rest at the Yellow Flower Temple half way to the village." So Ume-Hana had slung the strongbox over her back and set out for a long walk.

The midday heat on Grey Thrush Island is a fearsome thing. The sea wind, the breath of purity that protected all the islands, melted away. In her official robes, Ume-Hana felt like she was doing the same.

*　*　*

The promised path turned out to be little more than a game trail. It raggedly followed the lay of the land, adapting to the sharp contours and picking the easiest way through the temperate rainforest that made up the island's heart. For hours, Ume-Hana dragged her frame round moss-covered rocks, over dainty streams and through the tangled roots of trees so old that they had died and become infested with other species of climbing plants.

"All the gods, it's hot," Ume-Hana muttered to herself and continued her hike. Even the cicadas' chirping seemed lethargic and the forest constricted her.

She walked along the path which swung up and down the slopes, sometimes going quite high into the mountainous interior, at other places practically to the shore. As she walked, she got a glimpse between the thick foliage down into a small cove below. As she looked down, it became clear that there was something on the rocks. It was about the same size as a basking shark - shapeless, slimy, and it seemed to be pulsing at a rhythm quite at odds to that of the cicada's song.

As the path swung down into the cove, Ume-Hana decided to investigate. After all, she was a loyal agent of the state and it would have been remiss of her not to. She pushed her way between the ferns and shrubs onto the shore. Stones crunching underneath her sandals, she walked towards the creature.

It's a squid, she thought to herself. But far bigger than

any she'd seen before. It reminded her of the large shadow in the sea that she'd been so troubled by on her journey.

With her hand on the hilt of her sword, she edged towards it, trying to get a clearer look. Her precaution was unnecessary as it was clearly dying. It lay on the stones, flesh seeping between the rocks like rendered fat. Sphincters on its neck opened and closed with a wet, sucking noise, and its tentacles moved, rising up and limply dropping again.

Its monstrous form like a corpulent emperor was not what really drew Ume-Hana's attention, however. It was its eyes, huge and lidless. She looked into them, and they looked into her, observing her, her sword, her face, the insignia on her arm and the strongbox on her back. As she stared into their mournful depths, she became convinced that before her wasn't just some pelagic beast, but a divine creature in the final moment of its life.

She hung her head to say prayers for its spirit. As she began, a voice coming down from the mountains interrupted her; a clear and strong voice singing an old children's song.

My love has gone to sea,
To bring back crabs and fish for me,
But I must stay at home and pray,
That he'll return to me one day,
So now I wait upon the shore,
And nail flowers O'er my door,

"Oyy! Who goes there!" shouted Ume-Hana. She put her hand back on her sword. "Show yourself."

The bushes rustled, and a woman appeared squeezing between the trees with an ease at odds with her age. She wore a simple peasant's jimbe and no shoes. Her weathered hands leant on a bamboo cane as she picked her way down to the beach side.

She looked at Ume-Hana, saw her insignia and bowed in a panic. "I mean no harm, Official. I am Anu, a nun heading back to the Yellow Flower Temple," she said in a thick local accent.

"What is your business out of the temple?"

"I was visiting the head-woman at The Beak. I had a vision at the temple and it is my duty to report it to the villages. I'm just heading back now."

"A vision?"

"Yes, Official. I react well to the yellow flower tea."

Ume-Hana tried to scold the woman gently. "Well, be that as it may it, you shouldn't have been singing. A god is passing on." She wasn't to know that a portentous event was taking place.

Anu inspected the squid, then clapped her hands together. "I apologise, squid. If I had known, I wouldn't have disturbed you with my song." She turned to Ume-Hana. "What are we to do now, Official?"

Ume-Hana stood and thought; she wasn't completely sure herself. Her teachers back at the Daimyo's castle hadn't ever brought this topic up, so she improvised. "We should hold a vigil to honour its passing."

Anu nodded, sinking to her knees as you would in a temple. Ume-Hana remained standing with her thumbs stuck through her silk belt. The squid is a hunter, she remembered, a warrior's haughty stance is appropriate.

After two hours, the creature was done. Its flesh stopped heaving, the tentacles stopped their flopping, and the light went out of its bulbous eyes.

"It's over," Ume-Hana declared.

"It was well done, Official. Even gods shouldn't die alone."

It is too common a thing these days, Ume-Hana thought. She'd heard other stories of great beasts dead on the rocks of the archipelago.

"Official," Anu continued, "we should return to the path. It is a long journey to the temple, and the sun will set soon enough."

Ume-Hana agreed and they returned through the undergrowth to the little trail. They walked the path together, helping each other over the brooks, the roots of the dead trees, and up the steep rocky slopes. Light conversation bubbled out of Anu as she went. The life of a nun at the farthest, poorest peripheries of the empire was more than just sitting sedately and praying. They lived a life amongst the people, acting as healers, advisers, and ministering to their spiritual needs, not to mention mucking in when it was net repairing season or time for the harvest. Ume-Hana listened carefully, Anu's lively chatter lifted her spirit. She asked Ume-Hana lots of questions about the other islands and the Daimyo's court, apologizing with every question, explaining that she'd never left the island before.

"You know, Official, I should be quiet. I often talk too much, and if you want quiet, please say." Anu sounded suddenly worried.

"It's fine. I don't mind at all."

"It's just that I have a cause to celebrate."

"I don't see many reasons these days."

"It's hard to disagree, Official. The world has been out of order. Gods wash up on the shore. The men go out in the Iron Boat to fight ill storms, then return to the disappointed faces of their children when the catch isn't big enough."

Ume-Hana shook her head. Sympathy was an emotion she was becoming more and more familiar with. When she was younger, she'd had little time for sob stories. She'd put her thumbs in her silk belt and kept her head raised above the sufferings of the lower orders. That arrogance had gone with her youth and the sanctity of the sea. "So why are you happy?"

"Two weeks ago, I drank the yellow flower tea looking for an answer. I fell deep under its effect and dreamwalked for five days. My brothers and sisters worried that I wouldn't be returning at all, but I did, Official, and I found it out. The answer. It was revealed to me how to restore the sea, make it run pure and bountiful again."

"Oh?" said Ume-Hana, interested. It was a bold claim.

"The flower took me back into the past to when the waters were clean and the air didn't hang hot and heavy. There, in that place, I saw the corruption seeping into the waters leaving them barren, like you see today."

"What was it? The source?"

"Our Iron Boat."

"The Iron Boat?"

"Yes, Official, it's obvious. We never had these problems when the men rode the sea with the wind. It's these creations of metal and coal that have angered the sea gods and then drained them."

Ume-Hana stopped on the trail and thought about it. They were dirty, the Iron Boats, everybody knew it. "So, what did you do?"

"I told our chief. She agreed on her husband's behalf. When the Iron Boat returns it will be docked and the men will go out in wood again. There will be hard years to be sure, but the sea will return to us, and no more gods need wash up dead on our beaches."

"But don't you think..." Ume-Hana started.

"What's that, Official? I didn't hear you."

Ume-Hana didn't finish her sentence. The Iron Boats are bad for your health, she thought, everybody knows that. You stand on the decks, and you can feel it in your lungs. Sailors catch pneumonia and bronchitis. I've seen the poor houses where sailors died coughing up black gunk. But does Anu not know that the archipelago's Daimyo has over two hundred alone? A good amount of the taxes in my strongbox will go to making more. Retiring one will do nothing.

"Official?"

"Nothing... we should hurry if we want to make it to the temple before the sun goes down. You could sing a song. You have a fine voice."

"Of course, Official."

In the shadows cast by the setting sun on the un-dead trees, Anu sang another old dolphin-hunter's song. Silent tears ran down Ume-Hana's face.

Everybody knew, if they were bad for a person, naturally they were bad for the sea. But it was easy to not face the reality or dismiss it as somebody else's problem. The actions of one poor provincial island would change nothing. There was a puncture wound in the side of their vessel. It would take more than a single bucket bailed from the side by one small island to make it sound again, if that was even possible.

Ume-Hana flexed her shoulders, feeling the weight of the strongbox on her back. The Daimyo would have to do without its contents. She would donate it to the temple or give it to the villagers. Ume-Hana knew it wouldn't be enough, but they would need all the help that they could get.

The Necromancer's Garden

by Gerard Mullan

Still roses decayed on the vines. The garden's green was deep and brittle, shrivelled to the desiccated stylus of lifeless poetry, clinging to dry, dusty earth. Leaves rattled in the wind like haggard breath, calling for one last kiss from their lover suns. The light would not touch them. It dropped down, plummeting toward the garden, and then all at once twisted aside, condemning it to perpetual shade.

Gresha lay on the grass, her dress torn by brambles and ochre with dirt, a smile on her face any picnicker would happily return, one cheek itching manically from the tickle of grass. No—one returned her smile. She did not care. The lifeless grass clawed her through her clothes, threatening to draw blood.

She didn't notice.

Absently, she let her eyes drift in lazy saccade, and spoke to her garden of what she saw.

"The liddies are thriving," she said to their papery snouts. "You indiglots look so charming." They rattled, deaf echoes in their hollow bells.

Gresha's favourites were roses. They of all flowers seemed most amplified by death, their thorns blade—sharp, the red of their petals almost black. "You're beautiful," she told them, a tear leaking from her eye. "I could lose myself in you."

She almost did. Clouds swam across the sky, the suns arced, dusk came down in a haze of gold. All the while, Gresha was in her flow. She stared at the roses and wondered how long she might keep staring. She made it a game; once she stopped weeding details out of them, she'd head home. She remembered where she had found each of those roses, before settling them in the sheltered grove.

"You were from that night at the river banquet," Gresha recalled. "After I was betrothed." She chuckled at the thought. "That worked out well, didn't it? Mychelli, touching my hand in front of all those people and asking me to grow old with him, have his children, make him happy. Everyone was so pleased."

She frowned, recalling something she had almost forgotten. "He never wore his binding bracelet. He was looking for a reason to back out, I suppose. I guess I'm glad he did. It was a shame about the banquet, though." Out of the corner of Gresha's eye, she spotted a tendril of bright green sprouting from between the rusty blades of the lawn. She adjusted her weight, reached out two bony fingers and clamped them on the sapling, pulling it out by the roots. "Weeds." She pouted.

Shock punched through her as Gresha realised she had taken her eyes off the roses and lost her self—inflicted game. When she looked again, the shapes spun through their vines in the geometry of her mind had broken. She flopped on her back for a second, rocked her weight and used the momentum to pull herself upright, balancing on spindly legs. Her mother had once said her frame was ladylike. Her sister had retorted that Gresha looked like a spider.

"Next time, friends," she warned her roses, wagging a finger. "You can't win forever."

Dry silence met her, and she drank it in as others drink conversation, letting it fill her with cold vitality. As though oblivious to their sterile response, she brushed the dust off her skirts, smiled at the roses crookedly, and turned to pass beneath the stone archway of the garden's high wall. "I'll be back soon," she promised, reaching to stroke an outreaching vine. Gresha's fingertip met it with a snap as a twig broke away and fell to the ground. Humming, she left her garden and dragged shut its stone door behind her.

* * *

Up the path through the forest's pines Gresha reached her cottage, acutely aware that something was amiss. Her eyes passed indifferently over the bright needles of the surrounding trees and settled on the cottage's slumping frame. The grey slate roof reeked of rot and announced the house by the aura of its smell. But this was not what was wrong. She felt her steps cut into uneven blocks as she hurried closer. The floating pots that ringed the house and the desiccated specimens within them chattered in the low wind. But this was not what was wrong. What was wrong was that one of the bay windows hung smashed on its frame, and broken glass nestled in the white and fungal shrubbery below.

Gresha's hands balled into fists. Her jaw clenched as she marched up the steps to the front door and flung it open.

Her face hot, her limbs shaking, she sucked in a deep breath and approached the howling pandemonium of a full—blooded yell. But at its edge, her voice snatched. It felt like an explosion in her throat, held static by gentler instincts. She stumbled over the ragged carpet and stood framed by the door, fighting for balance.

"Who's there?" she croaked hoarsely, not recognising her own voice. Gresha felt the hideous bulk of a kha's presence moving through her home, occupying all spaces at once, the potential of its infection everywhere. She reached for the hand—rake she kept by the door with her other tools, knocking over the pot she kept them in. It rolled sideways and smashed on the floor.

"Gresha?" a voice called out. Recognition prickled through her, warping through the chimerical memories of her abandoned past.

"M—Mychelli?" she asked uncertainly.

From the left, in the narrow room where she kept her books and oddments, Mychelli appeared. He filled the gap between the slumping ceiling and the uneven floorboards, a shade immense. Gresha couldn't look at him, never could look at a face for longer than a glimpse before diverting her sight elsewhere. His shoes happened to be where they refocused. Snug black leather, silver clasps. The same high fashion to which he had always aspired. Mychelli changed his look, his clothes chromatophore and camouflage. Yet he was always, Gresha thought, exactly the same. The same demanding presence, being where it didn't belong.

"You broke my window," she said, still looking at his shoes.

"It is you," he replied, to himself. "I couldn't believe you really lived here, when I came up the path. Everything's dead, and that terrible smell... I broke in because I thought the place was abandoned. I thought I'd be able to find out where you'd gone."

"This is my home," she asserted. "It's mine." Her eyes darted to his face, and she saw the confusion there, glaring out of the hodgepodge kha—ness of eyebrows and lips and funny ears. Her eyes settled on the ceiling board above his head, on the knotted puddle of brown wood rippling through the lighter hues. How could she make it clearer to him? "You broke my window," she repeated.

"I'll fix the window," he said, his tone edged. "Look, forget the window." Something shifted imperceptibly in him, the colours of his clothes swirled. Gresha caught a glimpse of gold at his wrist. "It's so good to see you again! Everyone's missed you terribly. Your sister, your mother, me... none of us knew where you went. We were worried."

She raised a hand defensively across her chest, oblivious to the fact she still clutched the hand—rake like an extending claw. "I wrote a letter. Mother was screaming last time I saw her."

"Well, we were all screaming," he said, speaking to her as though to a child. "Didn't you see what happened? We were talking about the marriage, remember? Then the servants brought the third course, imported flax wine and pandragorum root. And then..."

Gresha did not have to look at him to ascertain his

discomfort. She knew what had happened next. She had been staring down into the shallow bowl before her, contemplating the broiled root with silent disgust. The pandragorum looked suspiciously like a mutilated corpse, sinewy threads jutting from bulbous limbs. Mychelli had been talking of baby boys, having enough of them to revive the names of a dozen bachelor uncles. Her gut had heaved. The pandragorum at each place setting had responded to her discomfort with sudden convulsion. They had leapt up at their dinner guests, ready to throttle them with their stringy roots. Chaos had ensued. Amidst shrieks and thrashing and accusations of wychcraft Gresha slipped away, plucking a single perfect rose from the bushes as she went.

"Well... that's all over now, dear. They caught the sorcerer responsible ages ago. Hanged him in Turbleton in the Shuwwir. Then it was just a matter of finding you, to let you know it's safe to come home. It was hard work, but eventually –"

"I'm not going back," Gresha said, not waiting for him to finish. "This is my home. I have a garden."

"Don't be silly," he said. "The weather here is terrible! Your garden is a mess. We'll come back with a couple of lads from the village, bring your plants back in wheelbarrows, if you like. But you can't stay here. It isn't healthy, living on this twisted heath, surrounded by decay. You can't do this to yourself."

Gresha shut her eyes. "I don't have to listen to you," she said. "I live here now. This is my place, and you can't tell me what to do."

"You're killing yourself," he pleaded. "You aren't well."

Why wouldn't he just leave? "I feel good here," she said.

He sighed and reached to scratch at his wrist. Gresha

looked and saw that he was wearing his binding bracelet. Could that mean...?

"I didn't want to bring this up just yet," he said. "But we're still engaged. That doesn't disappear, just because you ran away. I hear you saying you're happy here, but you were going to be happy with me, too, remember? That's why you said 'yes'. Maybe you don't want to go back to your old life, but it won't be like it was before. We'll have our own estate. We'll make our life exactly as we want it to be."

Gresha paused. She had wanted that. In part because it meant getting away from her parents, her mother's "sit straight"s and her father's endless parties. But also, admittedly, because Mychelli had asked. No—one had ever asked her, the younger daughter, the one whose tongue was crippled as some had crippled legs, whose eyes were wild birds, never resting on anything close enough to be touched. It was nice to be wanted.

But was it better than being alone?

"We don't need to make the decision right now," Mychelli said eagerly, sighting inspiration. "Let me stay a night. You'll see things better, once you've slept on it."

Gresha felt a tingle of uncertainty. "I don't have another bed," she said.

"Of course not. This place is uncomfortably small, but I saw a rocking chair behind those shelves. That'll do, at a push."

She supposed that it would be alright, if he really wanted to stay. She wouldn't leave with him—it was too late now to upset her rosebushes and dig up the other flowers. She gave the slightest nod and wandered off without another word to rummage in her dresser for a spare blanket. It would be nice, she supposed, to sit at the fork of the two potential futures for a time, and watch their branches grow.

Mychelli busied himself with picking up the shards of glass around the window, squatting uncomfortably on the tips of his shoes. He jabbered constantly, to Gresha's annoyance. She sat in her rocking chair and clutched her knees, staring at inconsequential peripheries within his aura, but never quite letting him get out of sight.

"It's lovely back home. You missed the Glimmerin Parade. The Canon permitted a troupe of jugglers this year, and it made for a spectacular show. Madame Gonquin said they were the finest in years. You don't get anything like that passing this far out of the way."

"No," she confirmed, not missing the noise of passing carnivals in the least.

"It must be boring. Only these few books, no music or conversation to pass the time—I wouldn't have been able to sit still at all. You must be aching to get out and do something."

"I have a garden," she replied.

"Yes, you have a garden," he repeated. "Frondwort and mewgrass and pricklebush, I expect. I can't imagine anything much growing here."

She shut her eyes, wishing he would go away. "There are flowers," she said. She imagined the roses, crawling over the walls. "They're dark, and beautiful. I like looking at them sometimes, seeing how they move over one another, slow and gentle, and it's peaceful. I like it when the world's like that. Everything has its own place." She opened them, and caught a snapshot of the strange, twisting look on his face. Her eyes darted away.

"That must be the most I've ever heard you say at once,"

he said, scraping loose the shards clinging to the window frame. "You should talk more. You must think a lot, being so quiet all the time. People want to hear what you're thinking." Something moved inside of her, uncoiling, relaxing. "So long as it isn't morbid, or rude. But talking gets easier when you practise." It quivered and died.

She shifted in her chair. "I'm going to bed now," she told him, standing abruptly.

"Really? We haven't even had dinner! Aren't you hungry?"

"No," she replied, looking down. She left him at the window and retreated to her bedroom. Before climbing beneath the quilts on her lumpy bed, she took three jars from her windowsill and stacked them one on top of the other in front of the door. She didn't want Mychelli walking in while she was sleeping. Her sister told her boys would do that, sometimes.

She dug a hand under her pillow and pulled out a papery collage of dead leaves. Their damp, bitter aroma filled her nostrils, and carried her off into the forest. She traced the lines webbing across them as though they were the words of a love letter lost in time, rich in the shadowy substance of memory. Their tips twitched as she stroked them.

Drifting off, it occurred to her Mychelli might be hungry himself, and she had not shown him the larder. But Mychelli was smart and would take whatever he wanted. She could always count on people doing that.

Twitching her fingers, her lips in silent motion, she fell into uneasy sleep.

* * *

When she woke the next morning, it took a moment to remember there was someone in her cottage. She started at the thought, gathered the leaves from her mattress and shoved them back under her pillow. She moved the jars and crept with slow dread across the hall. Mychelli was sitting on a stool by the cracked black stove, burning a pan of scrambled eggs. He took one look at her and laughed. Her vision whirred and refocused on the coal fire and the crackling lumps within.

"Your hair's a nightmare! It's all frazzled. Have a look in the mirror, before it settles."

"I don't have a mirror," she said, reaching to pat down her hair.

Mychelli grinned, staring mercilessly. "I made you breakfast," he said. "Don't tell me you're not hungry, you have to be after skipping supper last night."

"I am hungry," she agreed. She fetched a pair of cracked plates and bent forks from beneath the washbasin and held them out for the eggs. Mychelli dished them over into equal heaps, leaving a runny residue in the pan. She went to sit and eat in her rocking chair, and Mychelli followed her.

"I thought it over, and I reckon we could be back home in a week," he said through a mouthful of egg. "We can get a carriage in Jaquenham. It isn't that far, once we get to the northern road."

"I won't leave my garden," Gresha replied at once. He needed to understand that. But somehow, it was still lost on him.

"Yes, I didn't forget," he said. "I'm sure we can put your favourite flowers in some of these old pots and take them with us."

"No," she said. "They need to be together." In the earth. In this place. Why wasn't that clear to him? It was so obvious she shouldn't have to say it. If she said it, he'd get mad, and he'd shout, or throw something, or break another window. It was the sort of thing you had to hear from yourself. If she said it it would be morbid, or ugly, or rude. If it came from him, he'd accept it at once.

Mychelli sighed again, with the same dramatic edge she was sure he conserved for children throwing tantrums. "We'll go down to see your garden then. Maybe there's something else we can do."

Gresha was unsure and finished her breakfast in silence. She did not want him there, or to have the memory of him linger there for the rest of her life. But she knew he wouldn't leave if he didn't see it or know how happy it made her. She would have to be brave.

She'd have to let him in. Then he would leave her be, and she could move on with her life. Mychelli would find another girl to marry, who talked about everything he wanted to hear and gave him a litter of baby boys who would grow up to be just like him. And she would have her garden.

She took his plate and put the dishes in the basin. "Come," she said, her eyes scanning the line of his clothes, which had changed again, their embroidery in swirl.

He followed her as she left the cottage and walked determinedly down the path. He spoke, and she ignored him, his words jangling about him like bells he used to announce his presence.

Deeper in the woods, between a spread of pines, the cracked and crumbling wall of her garden rose from the earth and loomed like the exposed fossil of something ancient, dead and powerful. Mychelli stopped.

"It's here?" he said. "In this ruin? We shouldn't be here, Gresha, it could be dangerous. Horrible things live in ruins. Bandits and ghosts and wolves and things."

"It's just a garden," she said, reaching for the mossy door. It usually took a shove to open properly, but today it had jammed shut, and didn't move when she pushed. "Help," she said.

He took a hesitant step, and then leaned against the door with her. "We should go back. I can get you more flowers."

"No," she said.

The archway yawned as the stones beneath it scraped loose from the desiccated earth. Gresha hurried inside, her feet prickling pleasantly on the serrated grey lawn.

The roses seemed to turn towards her, and the wind shook a death rattle from the hanging bells of dried up leaves. They were gorgeous, quintessent, spectacular– in their quiet, accepting way. Better friends to her than Mychelli ever could be. They loved her in a way she had never felt from anyone. Not for being a daughter, or a sister, or a fiancée, but for being herself.

She whirled to see him, feeling for once the courage to look straight at him. He was pale, his lips thin, disapproving, ill. He looked left and right, from the stagnant black pond by the silverdrops to the trellised castle of her prized sanguine roses, creeping up their vines. To see the disgust cut into his face ripped the smile from hers.

"This is my garden," she said solemnly, knowing he would never understand.

"It's... putrid," he wheezed. "Divines, the stench of it... the decay..."

"Sweet perfume," she said, taking in an intoxicating breath. "Everything smells sweetest, when it's dead."

"It's wrong, Gresha," he said walking toward her, one hand raised before his face, as if to disperse the hot waves of undeath, and the sight of the skeletal plants. "You're not well, we need to leave." He reached out to grab her hand and she pulled it back sharply, slapping his away. The sudden, brutal contact made her heart shudder.

"Don't touch me," she said, panic edging her soft voice harder and louder, like a dagger rising in her throat. "You can't say that to me here. You can leave, Mychelli, but I'm staying. You understand that? I'm staying." She trembled, scared not of Mychelli, but the urgent pressure building in her gut. Mychelli lurched forward again and grabbed her wrist before she could dart away.

She shrieked. "NO!"

"You can't!" Mychelli hissed through bared teeth. The face she had never been able to look at was sucking her in, a maw of ivory and shining white eyes. "This garden is making you sick. You'll die out here alone. Your family wants to look after you, they love you." She dropped her knees, sinking down into the scratchy grass.

He tugged and began to drag her toward the open door. She started to cry, unable to help herself. "Listen to me, I'm your fiancé–your friend. Doesn't that mean anything to you? You can't just say 'no' to this. You can't choose to be sick, you don't get to kill yourself. You've got to get better, Gresha. We can fix this!"

The panic smeared across her eyes like an oil slick, darkness blossoming over blazing brushes of white and green. Her legs were cut and bleeding, scratched open by the lawn. Her crying cut off with a shuddering moan;

another sound was coming to the fore. A rustling. The high wind. The angry discourse of her garden.

Mychelli dropped her hand.

She snatched it to her chest and curled up into a tight ball, rocking slightly, her hands sticky with the blood smeared on her shins. She did not want to look. He made an odd noise of alarm, a "Ha—" that cut off immediately. He fell to the ground next to her. She felt that new magnetic need to find his face.

Her eyes cracked open and she saw him, flailing soundlessly as he struggled with a legion of twisting black vines that tethered his limbs. She saw the dishevelled mop of his hair, and the thin tendrils running through it like fingers. From the mad flail of branches through the air she saw a twist of a stem, and a blossoming red rose turning toward her, its hypnotic petals an eye looking down into hers.

* * *

"I love the colours this year," she said softly to her garden.

"I love you every year."

As she walked around the circle of the lawn, fingers splayed to touch the petals of flowers as she passed, she imagined that their heads turned to follow her, talking back to her in their own rustling tongue. She stopped at the pond. She always stopped there, just in case she might see. Once in a while, Mychelli's face would stare up at her from the eutrophic depths, blank and still, with a thoughtful acceptance he had never had in life.

"I like you better this way," she admitted to the body

in the black waters. Then she walked on, toward her roses, who had more life in their still stems than she had ever found in all the rotten people she had once known.

Fathom

by J. S. Rogers

"Here we go," Dr. Hirsh murmured as her submersible, the Trident, slipped below Panthalassa's waves. The dropship that delivered them from the Hermes, the great research vessel in Panthalassa's orbit, retreated immediately up through the planet's thin atmosphere. The Hermes, too large to conduct close research on its own, lingered above Panthalassa, waiting for the Trident's crew to complete their research on the watery planet.

View-screens came to life around the Trident's forward compartment. Flickering, they displayed feed directly from dozens of tiny cameras around the Trident's outer hull. "We were right about the colors," Hirsh noted. The liquid around them contained countless hues, stirred by unseen currents, all shifting and moving around one another without blending together.

Hirsh tore her gaze away from the rainbow-filled displays and back to the inside of the submersible. Lieutenant Smith—tall and trim, with dark skin and hair dyed metallic gold—sat in the Trident's pilot seat, his hands steady on the controls as he leveled them out. "Pressure is as expected," Smith said, after flipping two switches and opening communication with the Hermes. "Drop is completed. Ventilators are functioning within acceptable parameters. Engines One, Two and Three are...." He glanced over; Hirsh flashed him a thumbs up. "Up and running. We're recording properly. No sign of lag. Radar's active. Looks like we're good down here, Hermes."

"Copy that, Trident," Captain Sing's voice echoed in the transmitter tucked against Hirsh's auditory nerves, deep in her ear canal. "Tell Dr. Hirsh to get this planet sorted out for us, would you?"

Smith grinned sideways across at Hirsh, his teeth gleaming against his dark skin. "I don't think I could stop her, Captain. Expect a transmission in an hour." He cut the comm and leaned back. "Well, Doc," he said, "you heard the Captain. Let's not waste any time."

* * *

Among all the planets Hirsh had seen, Panthalassa stood out as unique: a giant world covered in oceans with a strange, tiny core. It orbited so far from its old, dying red giant star, that, by all rights, it should have frozen over completely. Panthalassa's thick atmosphere, full of unusually high amounts of methane, water vapor, and carbon dioxide, held a lot of heat in close to the planet, but not enough to sustain the world's massive free oceans. And, even stranger, nothing larger than a microorganism seemed to live in the brilliantly colored oceans.

Hirsh had observed the planet for a week aboard the Hermes, while the crew of the ship completed their exploration of Panthalassa's solar system, before finally convincing Sing that exploring the strangeness of the farthest planet from the sun required boots on the ground. Or, more accurately, a sub in the ocean.

The Trident carried a crew of five, including Hirsh and Smith. Doctors Lopez and Sokolova, experts in marine planets, and Sergeant Jei Howard, an expert on the Trident's mechanical systems, rounded out the crew. The submersible was roughly twenty-five feet long, with a large back compartment and a smaller front compartment that could be sealed in the event of a catastrophic hull breach. Computers and lab equipment took up most of the available space, leaving barely enough room for the storage of packaged food and water. Squeezing past another person was possible, but space remained at a premium. Claustrophobics avoided missions on the Trident; Hirsh benefitted from her short, slight stature.

Hirsh stood in the area between the compartments to address the other scientists. They'd all worked together a long time on the Hermes, making the briefing more of a formality than anything else. "Alright," she said, "you've all got your assignments. We don't have unlimited time planetside, so I expect everyone to work quickly and accurately. Make no mistakes. Our findings are going to shape the understanding of this planet for decades, until another ship comes all the way out here to follow us up. Understood?"

"Yes, ma'am," excited Doctor Lopez said. The strangest things thrilled marine biologists. The crew immediately turned to their computers, and Hirsh left them to it. She took the time to pull her messy red curls up into a ponytail before returning to her station in the front compartment. The endless sea, colors changing for a reason she hadn't yet divined, waited outside the hull, over a hundred miles deep and full of possibilities. Hirsh cracked her knuckles and grinned.

* * *

"What've you found?" Lieutenant Smith asked, startling Hirsh. Their pilot was light on his feet, quiet for a man of his height and size. He laughed, patted her shoulder, and found a bare section of wall to lean against. "I'm about to make my report, but all I can tell them is that the colors sure are nice. Some specifics would be appreciated."

"The samples are strange," Hirsh said, leaning away from her holo-screen and gesturing at the molecular compounds displayed in three perfect dimensions. She'd never seen the carbon formations before and she'd explored over a hundred planets. Some previously undiscovered molecule had bonded to the carbon and resulted in a molecular shape she'd never seen. "And that's not even addressing the lifeforms that Doctor Lopez found."

"Lifeforms?" Lieutenant Smith tensed up. "Why wasn't I informed that you'd found life here? There are procedures—"

"Relax, Lieutenant," Hirsh said, waving a hand.

"They're microscopic. More like plankton than anything else. Just...."

Smith frowned. "Just what?"

"I don't know, it's just strange," Hirsh said. "We're not sure what they eat. Panthalassa is so far from the sun they shouldn't be getting enough fuel for photosynthesis based on their structures. And the concentration of them around the ship seems to be increasing."

"Maybe we taste good," Lieutenant Smith suggested. "Or maybe we're just passing through an area where they're heavily concentrated."

"Mm. In any case, they're not dangerous. I think we're ready to move deeper, if you could take us down after you've sent the communication?" As she spoke, the Trident rocked. Doctor Sokolova, their chemical oceanographer, cried out in surprise. Lieutenant Smith jumped towards the forward controls, with Hirsh following on his heels, her chair spinning behind her. For a second, she swore she saw something move on one of the lower view screens, something huge. But it had to be nothing more than a shift in the colors around the ship.

"What happened?" Smith demanded of Sergeant Howard. The mechanical engineer looked up from the pilot's seat, all the color drained from his completely hairless face.

"I don't know," Howard said. He cut a look towards the screens and licked his lips. "I know it's crazy, but I could have sworn something hit us. But that's not... I mean, there's nothing out there. Look." He gestured at the screens. "We must have hit a thermocline, or an underwater river."

"Move," Hirsh said, directing Howard out of the way and scowling at the recorded scans. They revealed nothing.

"Well?" Lieutenant Smith asked, leaning over Hirsh's shoulder. Behind him, the other three members of the crew clumped together. Howard tittered again, scratching at his smooth head.

"Nothing," Hirsh said, tapping a finger on the controls. She frowned at the view-screens. "There was nothing there." She sighed. "Take us deeper."

* * *

The water settled into purples and silvers as they dove deeper throughout the day, the crushing pressure of all the leagues above them blotting out ever more light. Contact with the Hermes grew difficult. "I think it's the organisms," Doctor Lopez explained, when Howard failed to resolve the communication issue. "We're still attracting large numbers of them. They might be impacting the transmitters."

"Are they going to affect any other systems?" Lieutenant Smith asked, twisting around in his chair.

Lopez shrugged. "They don't seem to be."

Smith sighed and looked over at Hirsh. "Let's just go a little deeper," she said. "We've almost reached our depth limit, anyway." The liquid outside shifted colors, giving the impression of ghost-like movement. Hirsh rubbed her eyes, and the movement resolved into nothing but shadows.

* * *

Hirsh looked up from a sample of Panthalassa's oceans when the Trident shook. She grabbed for the sample with gloved hands and missed. The sample fell sideways into its intended case, but luckily stayed intact. The liquid separated out into individual colors, the tiny droplets trembling as the Trident lurched. "Smith!" Hirsh yelled over the shouts of the others. Her shoulder slammed into one of Doctor Lopez's stations. The Trident rolled.

"Not now!" Smith called back, as the rest of the crew hit walls, then the ceiling. Samples clattered around in their cases. Finally, the Trident settled, leaning only slightly to one side. Hirsh lay panting against a computer. The others moved around her, groaning and holding injured body parts.

Hirsh dragged the back of her hand across her nose, wet smearing over her skin, and asked, "What was that?"

Lieutenant Smith sat at the forward controls, buckled into his seat, scowling. Hirsh could have sworn something impossible moved across the screen behind his head. She checked the sensors to confirm what she'd seen and found them dark. Damaged. "I don't know," Smith said, hitting a switch. The Trident leveled out for a moment, before listing just slightly to the other side. "Something hit us."

Hirsh shivered. "Nothing hit us," she said. "There's nothing out here to hit."

"Alright, Doc," Smith said. "Sure. Well, whatever didn't hit us did some damage, too. Engines are down."

"What? All of them?" Hirsh leaned over Smith's shoulder, frowning at the controls for the Trident's propulsion systems. "But we're not sinking."

"We were," Smith said. "We reached an equalization point. The water below us is too dense to let us sink any farther. The hull's barely holding from the pressure, but we're not going to drop anymore, as long as the Trident maintains pressure."

"We're adrift?" Doctor Lopez implored, crowded in the

space between compartments. A smear of blood ran down from his temple. He spoke too loudly in the enclosed space. "We have to call for help."

Smith's frown deepened. "I've been trying," he said. "Communications are down."

"Well, launch the emergency buoy," Doctor Sokolova demanded, her face red and blotchy. "We can't stay down here. Not with that thing out there."

"There's nothing out there," Hirsh said.

Lieutenant Smith cleared his throat. "The buoy won't launch," he said. "The mechanism jammed."

"Shit," Hirsh hissed. Something moved on the screen, right at the corner of her vision, she could have sworn... Hirsh rubbed her head, frowning. She must have hit it when the Trident spun. "Alright. Fine. Howard, you work on getting us engines. Lopez, Sokolova, see if you can find out what really happened to us. Smith, see what you can do about communication. I'll work on freeing the buoy."

* * *

Half the Trident's systems failed to respond to any commands. Hirsh ended up pulling panels off the walls to access the circuitry below, attempting to reroute power around failing systems. The Trident slowly turned more onto its side. She found a damaged connection and reached for her tools when Sergeant Howard screamed, high and splitting. Something shattered. Hirsh dropped her work, ran towards the noise, and found Howard slamming a drill down onto one of the view-screens, over and over again. He managed to crack the screen, the image on it fracturing into a thousand pieces. Half of the shards fritzed out to blackness.

Lieutenant Smith grabbed Howard from behind, swearing and lifting him away. Howard thrashed, still screaming and struck Hirsh a ringing blow against the jaw as she tried to take the drill from his hand.

"That's enough!" Lieutenant Smith yelled, slamming Howard against the hull. The scientist gibbered as Smith dragged his hands back, one at a time, pinning them at the small of Howard's back and tying them with a zip-string. "Hirsh? You okay, Doc?"

"I'm alright," Hirsh said; her jaw throbbed, and her mouth tasted of copper. She knelt by the damaged viewscreen and shivered. Purple and silver filled all the other screens. Nothing moved. "You want to tell me what happened, Howard?"

"I saw it," Howard babbled. He'd gone limp and slid down the wall. "I saw it, I saw it."

"What did you see?" asked Doctor Sokolova.

"I saw it," Howard repeated. He rolled his eyes up to look at Hirsh. His pupils were huge. "I saw it. We're all going to die. It's going to kill us all."

Doctor Sokolova cried out.

"Stop it," Hirsh snapped. "There's nothing out there."

"He said—"

"There's nothing out there," Hirsh shouted. Sokolova and Lopez shrunk back from her. "You've all seen the scans. There's nothing here but us. Not on this entire planet. Everyone take a deep breath and let's get back to work. Lieutenant, could you...?"

Lieutenant Smith knelt by Howard, the medical kit in his hand. "Already on it," he said, flicking the point of a needle to remove the gas bubbles. "Shh, buddy. You're gonna be fine now." A moment later, Howard went blessedly quiet and limp as the sedative took effect. Hirsh stepped on a piece of the shattered view-screen when she returned to her work. It scrapped across the floor.

* * *

"Hey," Lieutenant Smith said, leaning close to Hirsh with a quick look to ensure the others weren't paying attention. Hirsh grunted a response. "So, communications are shot. Whatever the problem is, it's on the outside of the Trident."

"Of course," Hirsh grumbled. She'd arrived at roughly the same conclusion about the buoy but refused to give up. Smith shifted his weight from foot to foot, his arms crossed tightly. "What? Is there something else?"

Smith grimaced and bent a little closer. "Just," he said, "look, I know it can't be right, but I keep thinking I see something out there. Can you tell me…?"

Hirsh grabbed his collar, shaking just a little to make her point. "There's nothing there. I've done the scans a dozen times. We're alone. It's just the… I don't know, the pressure down here, or something. It's probably affecting the fluid in our eyes or pressing against our occipital lobes. Making us see things. That's all."

Smith nodded, closing his dark eyes for a moment. "Right," he said. "Right, thank you."

The Trident rocked again. "And that's just the current," Hirsh said, without looking away from Smith. "It's going to push us around more, now that we lost engines. That's all it is."

* * *

"Howard's waking up!" Doctor Sokolova shouted, tripping over her feet and interrupting Hirsh's work.

"He can't be," Lieutenant Smith said, as Hirsh pulled her arm out of the Trident's wiring, where she'd been trying to manually form a connection to allow for the release of the emergency buoy. "I gave him a full dose of Halo. He'll be out for at least twelve hours."

Sergeant Howard burst into crazed laughter, far too loud in the enclosed space of the Trident. Hirsh swore, wiped her hands on her pants and stepped into the back compartment. Howard remained strapped into his dropchair, his arms and ankles tied down. Doctor Lopez stood frozen on his far side. Howard swiveled his head around to look at Hirsh, and his laughter cut off abruptly. A wide, crooked smile remained. "You're all going to die," he said.

"No one is going to die," Hirsh said.

"I'll dose him again," Lieutenant Smith offered.

"It won't help," Sergeant Howard said, still staring at Hirsh, unblinking. "Nothing you do will help. You can't save them. It's going to take them all." He began humming, off key, and rocked back and forth.

"You can't give him more," Doctor Lopez interrupted, tiptoeing past Howard. "He could go into respiratory arrest. Look at him. He's already... not well." Sweat poured down Howard's brow, despite the chill in the Trident. A bright red flush crept up from below his uniform, and his eyes glazed over.

"Shit," Hirsh murmured, tugging at her hair. "He's right. And Howard can't... hurt anyone. So just try to ignore him, alright?"

Howard's renewed laughter, cracking and loud, followed Hirsh back to the front compartment.

***

Exhaustion settled over the crew as the hours dragged by. "I can take watch while you three sleep," Lieutenant Smith offered, after catching Hirsh yawning for the fifth time. Howard had quieted, only murmuring senselessly, making the Trident almost peaceful.

"Thank you," Doctor Sokolova said, "we'd appreciate that."

"Watch for what?" Hirsh asked.

Smith shrugged and tossed Hirsh a sleeping pad. She unrolled it in the cramped space within the front compartment, where she could listen to the faint hum of the computer processors. She turned, again and again, putting both of her arms under her head, before finally sitting up. The noise of the ocean echoed through the hull, strange and gurgling.

Impossible.

The Trident's hull was two feet thick. She pushed her back against the hull and focused on the sound of her heart. "Doc?" Lieutenant Smith asked.

"I hate these," Hirsh complained about the pads. "I'd rather sleep in the chairs." She climbed into her chair, pulled her legs in and curled up. For a second, before her eyes shut, she swore she saw something huge and dark pass across one of the screens, but exhaustion overtook her before she could identify it.

***

Doctor Sokolova's screams woke Hirsh from a dream about cold water, and the smell of salt. Sokolova stood in the rear compartment of the Trident, pointing forward at the view-screens, tremors wracking her body. Nothing but purple filled the screens. "I saw it," she yelled, her voice breaking, as Doctor Lopez moved to grab her. She dug her fingers into his arms. "I saw it, I saw it, I saw it."

"You were dreaming," Hirsh told her.

"What did you see?" Doctor Lopez asked. "Shh, shh, what did you see?"

"The eyes," Sokolova said, sagging as her knees gave. "I saw the eyes." She looked at Hirsh, dreamy, her face slack, and her pupils so wide the green of her eyes had disappeared. She exhaled a shuddery laugh. "And it saw me." And she reached up, lightning quick, her fingers hooked like claws. She didn't even blink as her nails reached her eyes.

"No!" Lieutenant Smith yelled. Lopez tackled Sokolova sideways, grabbing for her wrists. Her hair fell forward. Dark blood slid down her fingers and across the angles of her face. Hirsh's gorge rose. She reached out and held onto the wall.

Beside them, Sergeant Howard burst into crazed laughter.

***

"Lopez says we might be able to save one of her eyes," Lieutenant Smith said, after restraining Sokolova. He collapsed into the pilot's seat. "If we get out of here soon."

Hirsh tossed aside the tiny soldering iron in her hand, and thumped her back against the computers, avoiding so much as glancing at the screens. The purple no longer appealed. "She—" Hirsh started, then bit her tongue.

"I know," Smith said.

"I have to find a way to activate the buoy," Hirsh grunted, turning back to the computers. She felt the view-screens. Watching her. "Turn off the screens," she ordered, shuddering. Bad enough they had to listen to Howard's crazed gibbering and Sokolova's sobs. They didn't need to look out into the endless colors as well.

"You got it, Doc." A moment passed. Purple light continued to bathe the ship. "Hirsh," Smith said, quietly. "They won't turn off."

"What?" Hirsh leaned across Smith, activating controls while keeping her head ducked away from the screens. "All you have to do is...." She trailed off, the controls dead and useless under her hands. "I don't understand," she said, going through the procedure again and again. "I don't —? Why won't —?"

Smith grabbed her wrists, his calloused fingers soft against her skin. His expression looked grim. She focused on his eyes, not the screen behind his head, not the movement she knew she saw. "It doesn't matter," he said. "Just get that buoy working. Okay?"

"Right," Hirsh said, nodding. "Right. I don't have time to worry about a stupid glitch." Smith stood. "Where are you going?"

"For blankets," he said and when he returned he covered the screens as best he could. The purple bled through the fabric, along with strange, impossible shadows.

* * *

Weariness scratched at the back of Hirsh's eyes and fogged her thoughts. It took a sudden strange quiet from the rear compartment to rouse her.

"Wake up," she said, shoving Lieutenant Smith's knee as she stood. The dimmed lights, weakened by the drain on the Trident's power, illuminated Doctor Lopez as he bent over Sokolova. He sliced through the bonds around her wrists. "What are you doing?" Hirsh demanded, charging forward. Smith caught her back, his hand on his sidearm and his gaze on Lopez's blade.

"What I have to do," Lopez said, moving to Sergeant Howard, who stared up at the ceiling, clicking his tongue against his teeth. Sokolova slid down to the floor, fell sideways, and reached for her face. She began to laugh.

"No!" Hirsh jerked forward, and Lopez pivoted towards her, brandishing his blade.

"Ah," Lopez said. Smith held Hirsh in place. "It's okay. It's okay. I saw it, too. I understand now." Lopez giggled.

"What?" Hirsh demanded.

"I had to look," Lopez said. "I had to see it. I could hear it. Calling me to. I had to see." Sergeant Howard stood up beside him and rolled his head towards Hirsh and Smith. "It's going to be alright now," Lopez said. He smiled, wider and wider. "We know what to do. We're going to get out of here. We're going to get us all out of here." Lopez took a step in Smith and Hirsh's direction while Howard moved towards the back of the Trident.

"Stop right there," Smith ordered, drawing his weapon. "Both of you. Don't make me—" Lopez lunged at him. The sound of the gun going off in the enclosed space deafened Hirsh. She cried out and jerked back. Lopez glanced down at the wound in his shoulder and began laughing, high and cracking. Beside him, Sokolova staggered to her feet. Her face was a wet ruin. Hirsh slapped a hand over her mouth and screamed into her palm.

Howard reached the emergency hatch. "No!" Smith ordered. "Don't touch it!"

"He can't open it," Hirsh said, grasping onto that piece of logic. "The pressure is too—"

The hatch creaked.

Hirsh stopped breathing. The Trident rocked, hard. She lost her footing. Smith swore and grabbed her, dragging her body back into the front compartment as Sokolova and Lopez advanced towards them. "Close it!" Smith yelled. "Close it now!" He fired again. And again.

Hirsh scrambled at the door controls, sure that they would fail her as well, but they responded. She sobbed in relief as the doors hissed, sliding together and locking, just as Lopez lunged to grab her. She heard the crunch of his bones when the doors shut. A moment later the Trident jerked hard, thrown into a spiraling tumble as the emergency hatch blew, and the ocean had its wicked way with the rear compartment.

The spin threw Hirsh and Smith around, introducing them to every hard corner of the compartment, before slowing as the resistance in the water stopped their movement. They landed tangled together, blankets twisted around them.

"Don't look," Hirsh hissed, swallowing the gorge in her throat. "Don't open your eyes. The screens—"

"Shh," Smith said. "I won't."

"They opened the hatch," Hirsh whispered, after another moment. The slowed roll of the ship forced her up to her knees. She kept her eyes squeezed shut. "They... I don't understand. I don't understand." She heard the ocean, moving against the blast doors.

"It's okay," Smith said. He found her hand and squeezed.

"No." Hirsh shook her head and tasted bile. "No, it's, what if we—what if we see it? We're going to go crazy, the same way they did. How long until one of us opens the cabin?"

"I have more ties," Smith said, his voice trembling. "I bet we could find our way to the chairs."

Hirsh took a breath, shaking from the speed of her heartbeat. "You want to tie ourselves down?"

"Yeah, I guess I do."

Hirsh pressed her hand across her eyes. She saw the others behind her eyelids, laughing on their way to death. "Let's do it."

* * *

"Do you think we're still sinking?" Lieutenant Smith asked, later. Bonds held Hirsh's arms and legs tight to her chair. She twisted against them automatically. Her wrists felt sticky and wet. "I swear my ears popped. How much pressure can the hull take?"

"We're not sinking," Hirsh said, daring the words to sound believable. They'd lost so much of their oxygen along with the rear compartment. But if the Trident's hull hadn't given yet, it seemed unlikely it would. "The hull will be fine."

"It might not be so bad," Smith continued, quietly. "It would probably be quick. We might not even feel—"

Tears left hot tracks down her cheeks. "Shut up," Hirsh rasped.

"I'm sorry," Smith murmured after a moment. Something hit the Trident, spinning them again, leaving them hanging suspended upside down. The purple light in the room seemed to grow brighter, pressing against Hirsh's eyelids. It sounded like someone knocked on the hull, a cheery little sound. "Do you hear that?" Smith asked.

"No," Hirsh lied. She added, "Don't listen."

"I can't help it," Smith said, like an apology. "I can hear it. I think it wants me to look."

"No!"

"I can't keep my eyes shut," Smith said, fear soaking through each syllable. "Hirsh, Doc, please, I need you to help—"

"Look at me," Hirsh ordered, snapping her eyes open. She knew where Smith sat, better than anything. She stared at him with everything she had left and his eyes met hers. "Just look at me," she begged, "just keep looking in my eyes." She strove to follow the advice, trying to identify the spot where his dark pupils met his irises. She ignored the shapes moving behind him, the horrible, impossible things in the view-screens. Smith held her gaze. "Don't look away."

"I won't," Smith promised. And he didn't. They stared, and the Trident rocked again, hard.

The shapes in the view-screens disappeared all at once, leaving behind nothing but light. The Trident continued to shake, twisting them back right-side up. The view-screens failed, all at once, showing nothing but blackness as the feeds cut.

Hirsh screamed.

The shaking turned to banging. Her heart hammered against her ribs, intent on escape. The others had come for them, to drag them into the deep. Hirsh curled her fingers up against her palms until blood flowed. "I'm really sorry, Doc," Smith said.

And Hirsh's radio crackled to life, buzzing inside her ear. "—said this is Captain Sing. Can anyone aboard the Trident hear me?" Hirsh's breath escaped as wheezing laughter. She couldn't move her hand to respond and ended up listening to Sing's voice over the radio as the Hermes drew them out of the depths.

***

The servos controlling the doors whirred to life after a small eternity spent in the dark. Light flooded in and Hirsh hissed, turning her face away from it. Exclamations of horror washed over her.

Gentle hands brushed back her hair while someone else sliced through her bonds. A nurse knelt in front of her and someone threw a blanket across her shoulders. Hirsh met Smith's eyes across the sudden crowd. He gave her a small nod; she sagged down.

* * *

"We came as soon as you released the emergency buoy," Captain Sing said, later that day, standing in the sterile sick bay, between the beds assigned to Hirsh and Smith. She'd conferred with the doctors before coming to them and then listened to their explanation of what had happened with minimal interruptions. "You say it wouldn't deploy?"

Hirsh frowned. "That's right. I don't know. It must have come loose when the rear compartment opened."

Captain Sing nodded, tapping her fingers on the foot of the bed. A doctor strolled over and cleared his throat. "Alright," Captain Sing said, tugging her uniform straight. "I think that means enough for now. We can discuss the rest once you've recovered."

"Captain," Hirsh called, before Sing could exit the room. Sing turned back. Hirsh licked her lips and cursed her dry tongue. "What was it?" she managed to ask. "Down there with us?"

Sing's expression tightened, just a little. "It's not important right now."

"Ma'am, please," Smith put in from the other bed.

Sing stared for a moment. "Nothing," she said. "We found no evidence of anything but you."

Folk Hunters

By Kate Karl Lanier

Ansa was hunter first and prey second, but it always seemed to be the latter that brought the most consequences.

She crouched behind a travel information desk, leaning against the cold stone sides. The sounds of a crowd assaulted her ears, echoing in the massive train station. The station still glared a clean, shiny white despite decades of people traipsing through.

A shiver ran deep through Ansa's chest. It wasn't due to the chill from the stone.

Ansa peered around the TI desk. There was nothing.

Well, nothing dangerous. There were lots of things going on. All throughout the station people raced from train to train, metro to metro.

There were bored businessmen scrolling through phones, grungy farmers picking at their work clothes, and families pulling along too much luggage and too many children. Ansa had once been with a family like that. In this very station, in fact. Although she knew it was irrational, Ansa couldn't help but sift through the crowd to see if she recognized anyone. A friendly face wouldn't be amiss right now.

She frowned. No, it would be very amiss, she chided herself. She couldn't dare to subject anyone to-

There they were.

Ansa disappeared behind the desk again, water canteen smacking the stone with a loud ring of metal. Breath caught in her throat as she pressed herself into the desk.

Thump, thump, thump.

Her canteen's clang echoed in Ansa's chest with adrenaline-pumping thuds.

She waited. And waited. A train slid into place on the tracks and vanished again. Ansa swore mentally; she'd missed another one. But there was no chance in all of Pangaea that she was going to move out from behind that desk while Hulder were still trying to sniff her out.

"Ma'am?" The voice was accented and had a bored tone. "May I inquire as to why you are hiding behind my desk?"

"Nyet," Ansa said irritably.

"I speak English," said the man in his flat tone. "Please, come out."

"Not now!" she hissed.

"Then please tell me why you're back there."

Like hell.

"Ma'am, I'm going to have to call security."

Ansa spun, boot squeaking against the pristine tiles as she looked up at the rail station worker. "No. Please don't." She couldn't do that again. And definitely not with those savage beasts yawning at her heels. "I'm just... waiting for the next train, but I'm trying to avoid some people."

"There are other places to avoid people besides my desk." The man regarded her, weak chin tilted to the side and pink features expressionless. "Please remove yourself from my desk," he repeated.

"Really, I can't. They have this uncanny way of finding me. They've chased me all the way from the Japan station." Ansa gave a small smile, trying to look as charming as possible. "Any chance I can just wait for the next train here?"

"The next train doesn't come for an hour," sniffed the attendant. "You can take the metro. Or hide at... not my desk."

Going underground felt like a terrible idea, but Ansa didn't have much choice.

"Fine," she said. "But can I stay until the metro is in?"

The man sighed. Even his sigh sounded bored.

"Five minutes. Then you may go." He sat in a comfortable-looking swivel chair and began tapping away at his computer.

The five minutes dragged on, cold and loud. Time went slowly in train stations. It gave too much time for reflection, the white noise of business giving way to memories, regrets, fears.

Mostly fears.

One of the sounds stood out as a metro train pulling into place just a few tracks over, breaking up her thoughts.

Ansa leaned out from behind the desk, looking at the sleek, white cars. She looked up at the attendant.

"Thanks, moskal," Ansa said, letting a little irritation slip through her friendly tone with the slur she had learned from old Ukrainian friends. Then she ran off before she could hear his coming sigh.

Looking at the torrential sea of commuters, Ansa wished she had wings.

Sidestep a person. Slide through a wet patch. Leap the luggage. Down into the tracks and back out on the other side. Jump a fence, duck a family. Around the fat man, over the child, and through the open doors of the metro car.

Ansa slammed into a seat, her shoulder smarting against the plastic wall. She was pretty sure that her rear was smoking in the seat beneath her.

The car was empty, save for a black man behind her. She heard him shifting to look at the sudden intrusion. But Ansa was busy making herself small by curling up in the seat. No one from outside the car could see her in this position, hidden behind armrests and chair backs.

She hoped.

Assuming they didn't bother getting in the car.

She also hoped.

Ansa looked underneath her arm. She could just barely see the platform through the metro car door under an armrest. Foot-steps became thunder, breathing spanned eons. Every hour Ansa had spent on the run through Pangea's web of trains and metros compressed into a single intolerable moment.

Why wouldn't the door close up and the car leave?

Would a life of running be made worth it? Or did that life have only a few claustrophobic moments left in it?

Slowed down time always gave way to fear.

Thump, thump, thump. It was the thump of those terrible footsteps, not Ansa's heartbeat.

People milling. She should have waited behind the desk longer. People walking. Or maybe moved to another seat, even further from the doors.

Not people walking.

She curled tighter, holding back her breath.

It was a trio of Hulder. Pale white skin and black eyes. Horrible, horrible mouths. One was tall, one was fat, and one was just average. All of them were terrible. They walked along, inconspicuous. The Hulder had learned to dress like humans, masked as their prey, all of them in dark t-shirts and shorts that showed off the blue veins of their thighs.

Only one had a tail, black and white spotted with a frazzled, tufted end curling out of her cut-off denim shorts. Ansa shrank into a smaller ball.

Only Ansa could see them for what they were. And they only wanted Ansa. She was their prey. She was the last Folk Hunter, and Hulder never forgave the Folk Hunters for the things they saw. The Hulder never forgave the Folk Hunters for making them prey.

If it would bring them any consolation, Ansa would have told the Hulder she wouldn't forgive them either. Not for the things she had seen, and not for the Hulder she had hunted.

But lack of forgiveness didn't mean lack of regret.

They stopped, and Ansa regretted everything.

"Excuse me," one said. It was a natural sounding voice, one that didn't match that horrible mouth at all.

The man behind Ansa looked up. Ansa stayed frozen in place, her stomach like a glacier.

Thump, thump, thump.

"Have you seen a girl?" asked the tallest Hulder. "Big backpack, boots? She has blonde hair."

Ansa's fingers curled over the bandana she'd worn to try and cover up most of her blonde curls.

Damn it! They knew what she looked like! And this man was going to betray her.

A ridiculous thought--it wasn't betrayal if you didn't know the person. Betrayal was when you expected someone to protect you, but they put you in a world of danger instead. It was when you were supposed to be safe but were given over to the monsters. It was when the price for someone else's comfort was your survival and they decided to make you pay it. Betrayal is regret, it is fear, it is something you ponder when time slows. Betrayal is something you don't forgive.

Ansa had experienced betrayal a long time ago. This was just the inevitable end of it.

She would be the last Folk Hunter.

Ansa pressed her face into the crook of her elbow, the black behind her eyelids turning red from the pressure as she desperately imagined outrunning them.

She knew she could not.

The man shifted in his seat, boots scraping at the floor. The whole world swayed as the weight of the cramped car shifted.

"Haven't seen her," said the man.

Thump.

The pale trio walked off.

Thump.

"Where in Pangaea," one hissed.

Thump.

The doors slid shut and the train vanished into the underground metro system.

Ansa sat up, looking at the man with a slack expression. She could only see his beanie from this position.

Thump.

He turned around. "I guess they wanted you?" He had a small smile, hidden behind black scruff. The smile was shaky.

He'd seen them.

"Nope." Ansa let the backpack slide off her and into her seat as their eyes met. "Now they'll want you."

Thump. A pang of guilt as the weight left her shoulders.

But it wasn't betrayal if she didn't know him.

About the Authors

Alex Khlopenko is a writer and editor from Ukraine. He really has nothing better to do.

Anna K. Scott is a long-time reader of fantasy from the UK. She studied archaeology but decided to pursue her love of writing instead.

Anna Smith Spark is the author of the critically acclaimed, Gemmell and BSF awards shortlisted Empires of Dust grimdark epic fantasy series (HarperVoyager US/ Orbit US/Can).

Avra Margariti is a queer Social Work undergrad from Greece. She enjoys storytelling in all its forms and writes about diverse identities and experiences.

Brandon Daubs is a proud member of both the SFWA and the HWA and has been previously published in Grimdark Magazine, Dark Fire and 4 Star Stories, and the anthologies All Hail our Robot Conquerors and Knee Deep in Grit. His stories have won Honorable Mention and Silver Honorable Mention from Writers of the Future.

Daniel M. Kimmel is the 2018 recipient of the Skylark Award from the New England Science Fiction Association and a Hugo finalist for his collection of essays Jar Jar Binks Must Die... and other observations about science fiction films. He is the author of three novels, Shh! It's a Secret: a novel about aliens, Hollywood, and the Bartender's Guide, Time on My Hands: My Misadventures in Time Travel, and the forthcoming Father of the Bride of Frankenstein.

Daryna Stremetska is a 28-year-old sci-fi and fantasy writer from Ukraine who is particularly interested in how technology, pride and prejudices break us.

Eliza Chan writes about East Asian mythology, British folklore and madwomen in the attic, but preferably all three at once. Her work has been published in British Fantasy Award-nominated Asian Monsters, Podcastle and Fantasy Magazine.

Gerard Mullan is a debutant sci-fi and fantasy author doing his best to bring a little magic to the world

J.S. Rogers has been writing since she could get her hands on a pencil and paper. These days, she writes as a freelancer for her day job and pens fiction by night.

KateKarl Lanier is military kid who has lived all over the world but mostly on the internet. "Folk Hunters" was her debut short story.

Luke Frostick is British writer based in Istanbul and the editor of the Bosphorus Review of Books. This is his debut short story.

Michael Kellichner is writer and poet from Pennsylvania currently living in South Korea. His short fiction has been previously published at published in Black Denim Lit and

Trigger Warnings: Short Fiction with Pictures. Poetry has appeared in Farrago's Wainscot, the Fredericksburg Literary and Art Review, the Tishman Review, and the Tahoma Literary Review.

Monica Wang's fiction has appeared/is forthcoming in GHLL (Pushcart nom.), The Temz Review, and Gallows Hill Magazine, among other publications. She spent her childhood in Taichung, Taiwan, and Vancouver, Canada, and now writes in Germany.

Olivia Hofer is a gay writer and editor of Three Crows Magazine. She is originally from Switzerland, currently living in England with her partner.

RJ Barker is a multiple-award-nominated author of The Wounded Kingdom Trilogy, a softly-spoken Yorkshireman with flowing locks. He lives in the frozen north with his wife and son.

Stephen Couch is a computer programmer, an occasional cover band vocalist, and a lifelong Texan. Visit him online and poke him with virtual sticks at stephencouch.wordpress.com.

T.A. Sola is an environmentalist and writer of speculative fiction from Florida, where he lives with his partner James and two crazy chihuahuas.

Acknowledgments

Writing and editing are bound to be a lonely endeavour. But producing a literary magazine and a short story anthology are not.

This has been a tremendous collective effort and a showcase of solidarity among people who believe in the power of stories.

Year One - a collection of short SFF stories would never be possible without the wonderful people behind the Three Crows Magazine - Dan Stubbings, Michael Roe, Anushka Bidani, Julie Rea, Ana Childe, Alexander Pyles, Casey Reinhardt, Anthony Perconti, Vicky Brewster, and Ray Gustavez. Without their help I wouldn't be able to select brilliant stories for the magazine and gather them in one place here.

A separate thank you to my colleague and partner -in-crime - Olivia Hofer. I can't imagine Three Crows without her and her sophisticated taste, an eye for a great story, and unlimited patience for my nonsense.

It would be unlikely that we would pick up without the people who believed in us for some reason. Thank you Anna Smith Spark, Michael R. Fletcher, Adrian Tchaikovsky, RJ Barker, Gareth L. Powell, Steven Erikson, Sarah Chorn, Alicia Wanstall-Burke, Lee C. Conley, editors of Unsung Stories, Radix Media, and Adrian Collins. Their support and advice means everything to me.

We would be nothing without Cze Peku's imagination and vision - they visualized our best stories and created the tone and atmosphere of Three Crows Magazine.

With each issue and each next anthology there will be more and more people to thank and that's great.

Ah, almost forgot.

Dear reader, thank you for picking this up and staying with us. There's more from where this came from.